DALTON

A SAVAGE KINGS MC NOVEL

LANE HART

D.B. WEST

COPYRIGHT

Edited by: All About the Edits
Cover by: Marianne Nowicki of PremadeEbookCoverShop.com

WARNING: THIS BOOK IS INTENDED FOR AGES 18+ BECAUSE IT CONTAINS ADULT LANGUAGE AND EXPLICIT SEX SCENES.

PROLOGUE

Dalton Brady

"Now that we've got the name of the ATF agent investigating us, what are we gonna do?" Maddox, our newest patched brother, asks when all the Savage Kings are gathered around the long meeting table.

"We can't kill her or hurt her," Miles says as he lounges casually in his chair. "If she goes missing, that'll just draw more attention to the club."

"And hurting women is *not* what we do," War mutters while glaring in Miles' direction. Which is damn ironic since it wasn't that long ago when War had a woman bent over our table, whooping her ass with his belt. Not that she was complaining or anything, but still...

"War's right," Torin, our level-headed president, agrees. "So, how the hell are we going to handle this? Are we just gonna sit back and wait for Agent Bradley and the feds to bust in here to arrest us all, for who the hell knows what?"

"We need to find what she has on us," Chase, Torin's brother and the club's VP, speaks up and says from Torin's right. "If there's any evidence, we'll at least be able to hire attorneys to get in front of it."

"Reece, any chance you can work your magic on the computer to find out the details?" Torin asks.

Reece, our former military tech genius, shakes his head. "Nope. Already tried. I can't get past any big government firewalls unless I'm on one of their internal devices. But what I *have* found out is that this ATF bitch has been pulling public arrest records off the databases, specifically Chase, Abe, Miles, and Ian's. There was also a hit on Sax's marina and boat license files."

"Dammit," Sax grumbles. "If they bust me for the shit I do for the MC out in the Atlantic, I could get slapped with a life sentence."

"No doubt. Keep your boat in the docks except for recreational purposes until we know more," Torin orders, and Sax nods his agreement to hold off on his illegal smuggling and piracy shenanigans.

"What about a laptop?" I ask Reece. "Could you hack into their system with a government-issued one?"

"Possibly."

"If Agent Bradley has one that she brings home, I can lift it," I confidently tell the guys at the table.

"*You?*" Chase asks with a *humph* of disbelief.

"Yeah, me," I reply. "If she's looking into the Kings, she's seen the mugshots of half our guys and probably has all of the military records too. Maddox was the main contact for her CI we busted, so he's out. Sax needs to lay low, which means that I'm the only one without a criminal history or dog tags."

"How is it possible that your dumbass has never been arrested?" Abe asks me while stroking his long, black beard.

"Do I look like a fucking outlaw?" I respond with my arms spread out by my sides.

"Fuck no, blondie," Abe mutters. "Without any visible tats, you look like a California pretty boy who wears leather like it's a fashion statement."

"Exactly!" I say, not the least bit insulted since everything he said

2

is true. There's nothing about me that labels me an outlaw except for the words "Savage Kings" and bearded skull king tattooed on my back. Gesturing to my oddly perfect face, the one most men are so jealous of they try to punch it to make it a little less pretty, I tell my brothers, "This is my 'get out of jail free' card. I can use my ridiculous good looks to grab this chick's laptop, no problem."

Snorting, Torin turns to Reece and asks, "Do you think *Zoolander* here can really pull this off?"

"If I were a male model, I would be more like Hansel or Meekus," I point out with a grin.

Rolling his eyes, Reece says, "Maybe, if he doesn't get caught."

"I won't get caught," I assure them. Growing up as a teenager in New York City, the neighborhood gang bangers' vig wasn't cheap. If I didn't want to get my ass beat on the regular, I had to come up with enough stolen goods to keep the shot callers happy and off my back. Since my single mother was barely making enough money to put food on the table, I had to swipe a helluva lot of cell phones and wallets.

"All right," Torin agrees. "Then Reece, if you can get an address on this agent, I want you to go with Dalton to Raleigh tonight to start doing some surveillance. See if his sticky fingers plan is feasible without getting the club in any deeper shit."

"Sure thing, boss," Reece agrees before grumbling under his breath, "Lord help me."

"I refuse to lose this MC because some woman with a power trip and a badge put a target on us," Torin declares. "All in favor of the club committing a federal theft to try and save the Savage Kings?"

A chorus of "Yea!" is heard around the table, myself included.

My pop helped start the original charter of the Savage Kings MC. Hell, he's the one who carved the intricate bearded skull king logo into the very table we're sitting at. Rubin Brady was the VP to Deacon Fury and the two of them made the Kings a tight-knit family, one that spans up and down the East Coast and sprouts up a new charter every few years.

The MC is all I have left of the man my father used to be, so there's no way I'm gonna let the feds take it from me.

~

"Man, are you sure this is the right address?" I ask Reece from the passenger seat of his truck before crunching into another Funyun.

"Yes! And Jesus, brother! Out of all the snack chips in the world, why did you have to go and pick the loudest and stinkiest ones?"

"That's just how I roll," I tell him with a grin before chomping into another crispy onion ring, deliberately trying to make as much noise as possible to annoy him.

"This is why I prefer to hunker down alone in my hole in the basement and never leave," Reece grumbles to himself. Then he exclaims, "Finally!"

I follow his line of sight out the windshield. A tall, blonde woman just stepped out of the townhouse on the suburban street we've been staring at for the past eight hours. She immediately turns her incredible, round backside to us while she locks the door.

"*Dammmmn,* She-Ra is fine as fuck," I mutter because as the Commodores would say, Miss ATF agent is a brick...*house.*

"She who?" Reece asks, putting the binoculars up to his eyes before I steal them right out of his hands so that I can get a closer look at her thick ass. Not even the stiff black pantsuit can hide all of her voluptuous hourglass curves.

"Are you kidding me right now?" I ask Reece while watching the real-life version of the cartoon superhero walk towards her black Ford Interceptor SUV. "She-Ra was a big, beautiful warrior princess and He-Man's secret twin sister."

"Whatever," Reece grumbles. "Shit, I think there's a laptop in that leather briefcase on her shoulder," Reece says before snatching back the binoculars from me.

"How do you know?" I ask him.

"If you hadn't been checking out her ass, maybe you would have noticed that her posture is off. She's leaning a little to the right like the bag on her shoulder is heavy. And look at how she holds it delicately when she puts it in the backseat. That, my brother, is our jackpot."

"If you say so, Rambo," I reply before Reece cranks the engine and we pull away, following the agent's SUV downtown through rush hour traffic. He's good, making sure to put a few other cars in between us without losing her.

"Looks like she's going to work," Reece says after he slips our ride into a spot at the curb, half a block down from the federal building.

"Sherlock doesn't have shit on you," I tease him while watching her get out of her SUV through the binoculars before she disappears with her briefcase into the intimidating eight-story structure—a place where many criminals enter and very few seldom walk out without handcuffs and a long ass prison sentence.

"So, now we just need to figure out a way for me to get close enough to her to snatch the bag," I say.

"And how are you planning to do that, blondie?" Reece asks.

Putting down the binoculars to pull out my cell phone with internet I only use for personal shit and not MC business, I start typing away while telling my brother, "Give me a little time. I have an idea, one that never, ever fails."

"*Tinder?*" Reece exclaims when he leans over and sees the screen. "Fuck, man. You are out of your damn mind."

"I didn't see a man at her place last night or a ring on her finger, did you?" I point out while setting up my fake profile sprinkled with a few truths about me to make it sound legit.

"How would you know if there was a man? You slept the whole time."

Rather than argue that I was awake and paying attention more than he knows, I say, "Everyone needs love, right? Even warrior princess ATF agents with an ass that won't quit."

"Jesus Christ! You can't screw her, man!" Reece huffs.

"Why not?" I ask seriously, still typing on my phone.

"How about this," he says. "There's no way in hell that a federal agent would hook up with the likes of you. Her job makes her automatically suspicious of everyone right off the bat. She'll have you all figured out in an instant."

"Wanna bet?" I ask as I add the final touches to my profile. "A hundred bucks says I'll not only grab her laptop, but that I'll also be able to con her right out of her panties."

"Photos or it didn't happen," Reece tells me, offering me his calloused right hand to shake on it.

"Deal."

"There is no way in hell that you're gonna get anywhere with Tinder. And we need that damn laptop soon, like yesterday," he says.

"How would you know anything about the dating app?" I pause in my typing to look over at him. When the usually hard military man looks away, embarrassed, I say, "No way! You're on Tinder?"

"Maybe." He *humphs*. "But it's worthless. I've been on it for over a year and only had three matches."

"Seriously?" I ask, and he nods. "Well that's probably because you never leave the clubhouse basement unless ordered to do so. Let me see your profile."

He retrieves his phone from his pocket and then, after a few finger taps, offers it to me. Dammit, I try, but I can't help the bark of laughter that escapes my lips when I see his picture.

"Dude, you're bald in that photo! Chicks never swipe right for skinheads."

"What are you talking about?" Reece asks, turning the phone to look at it again. "I have hair. It's just all shaved off."

"Shaved so close that I can see skin! You look bald, bro," I explain.

"It's my Army photo."

"You need to take a more recent one, and preferably shirtless. The profile pic is the most important part of getting matches."

"Whatever," he huffs. "You don't even know if the agent is on the stupid app. And the odds of you matching with her in a city this big are probably like one in a million or—" Reece pauses mid-sentence when my phone makes a happy little chime. "What the hell was that?"

Grinning like the idiot I am, I turn the screen of my phone around so that he can see the confirmation—my face right beside a photo of the ATF agent. "It's a match, motherfucker!"

"You have got to be kidding me," he grumbles like a jealous chump, right before a rapid succession of more chimes start going off. Apparently, all the single ladies of Raleigh want to date me. Honestly, I could probably put down that I collect rattlesnakes on my profile and I would still get dozens of matches from my profile pic. My stupid perfect face is a curse.

When I was fifteen, I shot up to my father's massive height and build, but also inherited my Broadway star of a mother's too-pretty-to-be-entirely-masculine good looks. Ever since then, women have been trying to get me out of my clothes while men have been taking swings at me. Fifteen was also the summer my part-time pop started teaching me to fight. He knew I would need to be able to defend myself, and I have, aside from the one time I tried to run from a man with a gun and took a bullet to my back. The bastard almost killed me and came damn close to leaving me paralyzed.

So, yeah, I know for a fact that I'm not bulletproof like Superman. No, if I were a comic superhero, fighting and sex would be my only superpowers. Captain Panty Dropper to the rescue.

Hell, throwing punches and getting a woman into bed are the *only* two things that I excel at.

And for once, I can actually use those particular skills to help the club.

No one, not even an ATF agent, will ever suspect that a pretty, charismatic bastard like myself is actually an unrepentant thief who was born to be an outlaw.

CHAPTER ONE

Peyton Bradley

"Let's hear it. What's today?" Quincey asks, and I know she's not referring to what day of the week it is. She's a fellow government employee and my best friend since moving to the city a few months ago. We've just stepped inside our favorite downtown watering hole near the federal building for a few drinks.

Blowing out a breath, because the answer is so pathetic, I drop my black leather briefcase at my feet and climb up on the bar stool beside her to order a round of vodka martinis. "Day three-hundred and ninety-seven," I answer. "It's been three hundred and ninety-seven days since I was with a man."

"No! That's completely unacceptable!" she exclaims with a shake of her curly brown hair. "Do you really think tonight's Tinder match is going to be the one to shatter that record?" she asks as the bartender slides us our usual drinks.

"No way," I mutter, as I scan the men around the bar in search of my date and then look back to the door. "I have no doubt that I'm about to be epically Catfished. *Again*. No one is this hot in real life,"

I say. Pulling out my cell phone from my bag, I show Quincey the Greek god's face on the screen right when she takes a sip from her glass.

She chokes for several seconds, then swallows a few more sips of her drink before she's finally able to respond. "Wow. Definitely a Catfish," she says. "We'll never meet anyone half that hot in our dreams."

"Agreed," I reply with a sigh of disappointment as I pick up my own glass to take a sip. "The guy in the photo has to be a model or an actor that was screen grabbed from the internet, not the man who is supposedly just some local ambulance chaser attorney and loves Funyuns." I withhold from her the part of his profile that actually had me laughing at nine o'clock in the morning before I even had my first cup of coffee— the song lyrics proclaiming his love of big butts. The mention of the old-school song and mutual favorite snack treat are the only reasons I felt confident enough to swipe right on someone so obviously out of my league. If it is really him. Which I'm certain it won't be.

"Funyuns? Ew. I bet the real dude is actually old and balding, with a big ole beer belly," Quincey predicts.

"No doubt," I agree, since this isn't our first rodeo meeting men on the dating app. "That's why I wanted you to be here, so you can witness this epic train wreck in person."

"Wouldn't miss it for the world," Quincey agrees. "It sucks that all the men on Tinder are duds. Do you even remember what sex feels like? Or is it just a distant memory for you, like it is for me?"

"I sort of remember," I reply, as I cock my head to the side to try and recall the details of the last intimate encounter with my lying, cheating, son of a bitch spouse. "It's when you lie on your back and count the seconds, not minutes, that it takes for the relentless jack-hammer to stop pounding you into the mattress, right?"

Quincey actually snorts out a laugh before she says, "That's it! So you *do* remember your ex-husband! Honestly, girl, I don't think we're missing much."

"Very true," I agree. "My vibrator is available anytime I need it, and it's pretty easy to imagine that I'm with the hottie model from Tinder, even if I'll never—" My sentence trails off when the tinkling sound of the bar door opening grabs my attention. Then in walks... "Holy shit," I mutter. Slapping Quincey on her shoulder repeatedly to get her to turn around and look behind her, I say, "Quince, it's him! It's really him!"

"Sure, it is," she drawls sarcastically with a roll of her eyes before she cranes her neck around to see for herself. "Slap my ass sideways! I think he just blinked and put his baby in me!"

That's the moment when the gorgeous blond man in the navy-blue suit locks eyes with me from across the room and grins in recognition. As he comes closer, he not only looks at me like we've met before, but his eyes lower, taking in every inch of me on the bar stool and surprisingly enough, there's not an ounce of disappointment on his face.

"Peyton?" the hottie asks when he's standing next to me.

"Ah, y-yeah," I stammer. "That's me. And you're...*you*."

"Henry Aycock," he says, as he holds out his large hand and flashes me a dazzling, perfect row of white teeth. I shake his hand, even with my jaw still hanging open like an idiot. His palm isn't soft like most lawyers I've met. It's actually strong and calloused, like he's spent some time working with them. "And you're...even more beautiful in person," Henry adds, with a wink of one of his beautiful denim blue eyes that nearly makes me hyperventilate.

For the first time in my life, and despite all of my self-consciousness about my Amazonian size, I actually believe his compliment because he's looking at me like there's no other woman in the world. Or at least he *was* looking at me like that, until his eyes shift over to Quincey.

"And you are?" he turns to ask her while reaching to shake her hand. And no lie, she giggles when their palms touch.

"My friend Quincey was just leaving," I blurt out because it's been three-hundred and ninety-seven days since I was with a man.

While I'm not the type of woman to sleep with someone I just met, I don't want to lose out on the possibility. That is, if he's still interested in me. In person, maybe he decided he's not, and he's just trying to be polite rather than turn around and run.

"You brought a friend to meet a stranger," Henry says. "That's smart."

"No offense. It's just, well, I work with criminals every day," I say, to try to explain why I didn't trust him enough to meet him alone, leaving off the part about thinking he wasn't really the guy in the photo.

"Oh, right. You said you're an ATF agent," he replies. "The world's a dangerous place for a single woman," he adds coolly. "Quincey can stay if you would prefer..."

I'm shaking my head before he finishes his sentence. "You're fine." *Shit.* "I mean, I'm fine...we're fine. Quincey doesn't need to stay and babysit," I stammer, flashing her a pointed look that says, *please move your ass so he can sit down next to me.*

Grinning at me and then back to the handsome man, Quincey thankfully says, "That's right, I have to get going, but Henry, you should take my seat. It was nice meeting you."

"You too," he agrees.

Quincey then gets up, throws her purse over her shoulder, and brushes past him.

"See ya tomorrow, Quince," I tell her quickly before turning back to the sexy attorney. "Have a seat. I mean, unless you don't want to now that you've seen me..."

"Thanks," he says when he removes his black leather briefcase I just noticed was on his shoulder and climbs on the bar stool. In fact, it's nearly identical to mine.

Incredibly relieved he didn't feel the need to bolt, but not sure what else to say, I decide to point out the bag similarities. "Looks like we both have the same taste in briefcases."

"How about that," Henry agrees, lowering his eyes to examine the side-by-side briefcases. "My mother bought me this one for

Christmas. It was the last gift she gave me before the cancer took her…"

"Oh, wow. I'm so sorry," I tell him, since that's really freaking sad.

"It's okay," he says. "She was a good woman taken from us too soon."

"I'm sure she was."

"Anyway, I'm so sorry I was running late," Henry says, as he reaches up to loosen the knot of his tie. "I got held up in trial."

"Oh really? What kind of case?" I ask, picking up my martini and taking a sip to make myself stop staring at him.

"It's horrible," he says, and when I can't help but look at him again, his perfect face is pinched. "Little Jenny is only nine years old. She was getting off the bus when some idiot came roaring around it and hit her. The poor thing is now wheelchair-bound for life."

"That is awful," I agree.

"Don't worry," he says with a wink. "We're gonna get Jenny enough money to make her as comfortable as possible. I promised to take her to Disney World myself once we get a verdict."

"Aww, that's really sweet."

How is it possible for a man to look like him and then be such a sweetheart?

"Enough about me," Henry says as he rests an elbow on the bar and leans in a little closer toward me, close enough to trail his finger up the sleeve of my suit jacket. "I want to know about you."

"There's not much to know," I tell him. "I'm an agent for the Department of Alcohol, Tobacco, Firearms, and Explosives. My field office is in Atlanta, but the Eastern District needed my help on a few cases, so here I am in Raleigh, for who knows how long."

"How do you like it here?" Henry asks.

"It's nice and a little quieter than Atlanta." I examine his left hand to see if there's a tan line from a wedding ring. There's none. The guy is too good to be true. "My ex-husband is still in Atlanta, so it's nice to put some distance between us," I say as a segue into the subject. "What about you? Have you ever been married?"

"No," he answers. "First, it was all-in for law school, and then it took time to establish my practice. It wasn't until I lost my mother that I wished I would've settled down sooner, so that she could have met my wife before she passed away."

"Yeah." That makes sense. "Any...kids?" I ask, since you don't have to be hitched to make a baby.

"No kids," he replies with a grin. "You?"

"Nope. Not yet."

"But maybe later?" he asks, and it almost sounds naughty, like he's asking if I'm going to sleep with him tonight.

"Maybe later," I agree. "Just not too soon."

The truth is, I would break my own rule and take him home right now if not for my serious case of self-consciousness. It's just that this man is intimidating, which is a new sensation for me. I carry a badge and a gun. Not much unnerves me, but the Hollywood good looks and winning personality are too much. Before I sleep with someone of Henry's magnitude, I feel like I need to be more prepared, like with a full body wax or thousands of dollars' worth of plastic surgery. There's no way I'm ready to get naked in front of him, even if I really, really want to.

Would it be weird if I asked him if he had a tiny cock? Proving that not every inch of him is perfect would make me more inclined to end my drought tonight.

"Can I get you another drink?" Henry asks, as if he senses I need more liquid courage to just keep sitting here with him.

"Sure," I agree because I'm not ready to leave his presence just yet, even if I am out of my league. He's still here at least, talking to me, so either he's taking pity on me or he's still interested despite the fact that he's a twenty on the hotness scale of ten, and I'm only a six or seven on my best days.

The two of us keep up the small talk for an hour before I find myself getting far too drawn into him than is smart. I need to abort before I beg him to let me see him naked just once, even if he'll be disappointed in the quid pro quo.

"So, it's been really nice meeting you, but I better head on home," I tell him.

"So soon? I was having a great time talking to you."

"Yeah, I have to get up early for work tomorrow," I reply, warming all over because of his sweet words.

"Well, in that case, how about I walk you to your car?" he offers.

"Sure," I agree, even though I'm never concerned for my safety with all of the law enforcement and self-defense training I have under my belt.

I pick up my briefcase to grab the cash from my wallet, but Henry says, "I've got this."

"Thanks," I tell him and then hang my bag on my shoulder while I wait for him to lay down a few twenties and grab his own satchel.

"Ready?" he asks.

"Yes," I reply.

We walk in silence the few blocks to my black Ford Interceptor SUV that's parked in the basement level of the parking deck rented out to federal employees.

"This is me," I say, coming to a stop next to it.

"It looks...exactly like what I would imagine an agent driving," Henry tells me with a chuckle.

"Right," I agree.

I start to reach for the rear door to stow my briefcase when Henry suddenly says, "Wait."

When I turn around, he's digging into the front breast pocket of his suit jacket. He pulls out a small white business card and offers it to me. "My cell number is on here if you would like to go to dinner sometime?"

"Thanks," I tell him as I take the crisp card and read his name—Henry S. Aycock—and contact info written neatly in raised, golden font. "Dinner would be great."

"It was really nice to meet you," Henry says, taking a step closer.

"You too," I reply as I slip the card into the front of my pants pocket and look up at his handsome face. At five-ten, I'm almost as tall as most men in heels, but not Henry. I like that he makes me feel petite and delicate, even if I'm the furthest thing from that.

"Can I be honest with you for a second?" he asks.

"Ah, sure."

"I've been dying to kiss you since the second I laid eyes on you, but I don't know if that would be too much too soon," he says as his beautiful blue gaze lowers to my lips, causing my breath to escape my own in a gasp of surprise.

"A, ah, a kiss would be...nice," I'm eventually able to respond.

The words barely leave my mouth before Henry swoops in. I was expecting a soft, gentle goodnight kiss, but what I get is him pressing the front of his body against mine so hard that my back hits the side of my SUV. And then he's kissing me with enough tongue to make my panties instantly go wet from his unexpected show of dominance. His hand weaves into the side of my hair to tilt my head for maximum impact, simultaneously making my knees go weak.

It's the hottest, dirtiest kiss I've ever had, and I don't ever want it to end.

Letting my briefcase fall from my shoulder with a *thud* on the pavement that I don't even care about, I wrap one hand around Henry's neck and the other on his lower back to pull him closer, wanting to feel him. And boy, do I feel him.

He doesn't have a tiny dick.

No, he's thick and so long that the hardness in his pants stretches from above my belly button all the way down between my thighs.

Before I know what the hell I'm doing, I lift my left leg to hang it on his hip, practically humping him in a public parking garage. But it feels too good to stop. *He* feels too good pressed against me, hammering his substantial manhood between my thighs like he's just as desperate for me as I am for him. That's impossible, though.

Henry pulls his mouth away from mine on a groan then starts to kiss the side of my neck while we both pant, trying to catch our breath. "Stop grinding on me like that unless you want me to tear off your pants right here, right now, to give you every inch you're rubbing up on," he warns me, his voice deeper, harsher than before. "You've got five seconds to decide..." With a pump of his hips, he drives himself into me deeper, and I nearly combust on a whimper.

"Do you have a condom?" I ask, not even recognizing my own voice or the craving that's swept over me.

"Fuck yes," he answers, maybe even a tad too quickly. Of course this man carries condoms on him at all times. He probably goes through a box a week. But it's impossible to care about that right now with his damp lips moving along the column of my neck, causing goose bumps to spread up and down my arms. Embarrassingly enough, I even shiver. Never before have I ever felt this way—like I would die if this man doesn't do something to relieve the throbbing ache inside of me.

With his arm banded around my back, Henry yanks me forward to open the passenger door of my car. He kisses me deeply for a few more minutes before he grabs my hips and spins me around, putting my back to his front. His hands reach around and easily undo the front of my pants, then his big palm pressed on my upper back, guiding me down so my cheek is resting on the car seat. My pants and panties lower to my knees, the weight of my gun holster and badge helping with the rapid descent.

"Holy shit!" I exclaim. I was expecting Henry's cock, but what I got was the fluttering of his tongue on my hot needy flesh while one of his fingers teases my folds and then penetrates me.

It's been years, *years,* since a man put his mouth on me, and I don't remember it being this good before. Between my cries, I hear Henry's muffled moans that vibrate against my clit, making me think he's enjoying this as much as I am. He eventually removes his finger from inside of me to grip the front of my thighs. And then he's pushing and pulling my hips back against his face while thrusting his tongue in and out of my slick opening, simulating fucking me. It's incredibly erotic, so much so that it doesn't take long before my legs start to tremble right before they lock. Liquid heat explodes from deep inside of me, and then I'm screaming through the rush of pleasure coursing through my entire body.

Henry's tongue goes back to lashing at my clit until the tremors ease up.

"You were dripping wet for me," he says, before placing a kiss on the plump part of my butt cheek, and runs a finger up the crease of my ass lewdly. "Was that good for you, Peyton?"

"God, yes," I moan, unable to lift my head or move my weak limbs just yet.

"Glad to hear it," he replies with a chuckle as he removes his hands and mouth from me. There's a crinkling sound like a condom wrapper, then Henry says, "Ready for my cock?"

"Can't wait," I admit honestly.

"Let me roll this rubber on, and then I'm *really* gonna make you scream."

Instead of innuendo, his words sound almost...ominous. That's the first moment I start to think this—fooling around with a strange man—may have been a mistake, no matter how hot he is. I start to get up and call it good for the night right then and there, but realize that would be pretty messed up to give him blue balls after he gave me an incredible orgasm. So, I lie still and wait in the silence for him to fill me. Maybe he only meant that the sex will be better than the oral. I'm sure that's all it was...

I keep waiting, but Henry doesn't say anything else or touch me again.

"Everything okay?" I ask before I look over my shoulder...and see nothing but the car parked a few spaces down from my SUV. "Henry?"

When there's no response, I push myself up and finally straighten to look around the garage while quickly pulling my panties and pants up my legs. "Henry?" I say again, but there's not a person in sight. God, how embarrassing. I was bent over with my ass out and anyone could've seen me.

And what the hell happened to Henry?

Did he change his mind? Was it something I did?

Not wanting to wait around any longer, looking like an idiot, I grab my briefcase to throw it in the backseat so that I can get out of here, but it feels...incredibly light.

Oh no. Lifting the bag onto the passenger seat, I jerk on the zipper to open it and find nothing but a blank notepad inside.

Shit!

Not only did Henry bail on me, but he grabbed my briefcase instead of his!

CHAPTER TWO

Dalton

I could've fucked her.

I knew from the moment I kissed her that she would let me do anything I wanted to her. God, her tongue plunged into my mouth with a desperate urgency that was contagious. I already wanted her, but once she got my blood flowing south, I had to get on my knees and taste her. Just putting her face down on the backseat would've been enough of a distraction for me to snatch her bag and run, but I couldn't resist getting her off with my tongue at least once. Hell, I still can't believe she was bent over, naked from the waist down with a glistening pussy, ready for the taking...and I walked away.

Licking my lips that still hold her delicious flavor, I realize that tonight may be the first time I've ever turned down a willing woman. But it just felt wrong to screw her before I screwed her over. That would be too much like taking advantage of her, and I swore that I would never do that to a woman. Casual sex? Hell yes. I'm all for one-night stands. But I'll never use someone just because I can. Years ago, I was on the receiving end of such a shitty arrangement and I still haven't gotten over it.

While I'm still hurrying back to my bike that's parked a few blocks away from the bar, my burner phone starts vibrating in my pants pocket. I groan when it rouses my already hard-as-steel dick.

I can take a guess who is calling, since I used my actual number for the phony business cards.

The damn buzzing starts and stops against my aching shaft two more times before I've stowed Peyton's briefcase in my saddle bag and hit the highway, riding east back to Emerald Isle.

It doesn't take a genius to figure out what her voicemails will say, yet the first thing I do two hours later, after I back my bike in at the clubhouse and climb off, is hit play.

"Henry, hi. It's Peyton. I'm not sure what happened, or why you left so suddenly, but you grabbed my briefcase by accident. Maybe we can have coffee in the morning to switch? Please call me back tonight at 404-555-5899. Thanks."

Her voice is pleasant, with a hint of self-consciousness and an edge of panic that increases on the next message.

"Henry, it's Peyton again. There's a very important, government-issued laptop in my bag that I need back ASAP. The files on it are extremely confidential and about ongoing investigations. If you'll call me back and let me know, I'll come to your place tonight to pick it up and give you yours. Thanks. I'm waiting for your call."

The third message loses all hints of pleasantness and is downright rude.

"Henry, if that's even your real name, it's Peyton again. Did I mention that I'm an ATF agent? Right, well, funny thing, I did a search with the state bar and your name is not listed as being a licensed attorney. You don't come up when I do an internet search either, unless you're the retired, sixty-year-old Henry Aycock in Alabama. Stop being Ay-dick. Call me back so I can get my briefcase tonight!"

And the fourth and final message is straight-up hostile.

"Listen, asshole. I will find you and when I do, you're gonna be sorry!"

There's a hint of desperation on the last one. Her voice trembles like she's tearing up, even though she's trying her best to sound threatening.

I'm still thinking about her words when I walk into the *Savage Asylum.*

A manicured hand with bright red fingertips reaches for my arm, stopping me in my tracks as I start toward the basement door.

"Hey, handsome. You look mighty good in a suit," Alicia, one of the club regulars, says when I turn to face her.

"Thanks," I reply.

"But I know you look even better out of it," she replies with a wink. "Want me to come help you take it off?"

Even after the long drive, my dick is still looking for some relief, wanting me to finish what I started with Peyton. But I'm not ready to get rid of the agent's taste on my lips, or her sweet, peachy scent that's lingering on my clothes just yet.

"I think I'm just gonna crash tonight," I tell Alicia, blowing her off and heading down the stairs to my apartment with Peyton's briefcase.

Hell, maybe I'm coming down with something, turning down two women in one night. My skin underneath the suit and tie does feel like it's overheating. Nah, that's probably just the leftover effects from getting so worked up in the parking garage and having to walk away.

That's when it hits me that the feverish sickness that's come over me isn't from the hot make-out session. Instead, I'm pretty sure that it's...guilt. Guilt for kissing and touching a woman under false pretenses, knowing I was going to screw her over.

The culpability is a new sensation for me since my goal in life for the past eight years has been to never let myself feel anything again for a woman.

Peyton

"That son of a bitch!" I exclaim as I stomp around Quincey's apartment bright and early the next morning, with still no response from the jerk. She's in her green flannel pajamas, curly brown hair an enormous crow's nest, with squinty eyes, since I knocked on the door and got her out of bed before sunrise.

"I still can't believe he went down on you in what you claim was the best oral sex ever and then stole from you," she says between yawns from her seat on the sofa. "It was probably an honest mistake and he'll realize it when he opens up the briefcase."

"See, that's what I thought at first too," I respond as I continue pacing back and forth in her living room. "But my bag was so much heavier than his. He had to have known!"

"Okay, but why would an attorney rob you for a laptop?" she asks with her brow creased in confusion.

"He's not an attorney!" I shout, making her flinch. "He lied about that, about everything! And I'm gonna have his ass thrown in jail! Just as soon as I figure out who the hell he is..."

God, it's so embarrassing to even think about how stupid I was to believe a man I met on a dating app was who he said he was. Then, to not only let him kiss me, but more. What the hell was I thinking?

I'm pretty damn smart most of the time. I have a master's degree in criminal justice for chrissake. But being divorced and single for so long has apparently made me stupid when it comes to my personal life. Now a single moment of idiocy is going to royally screw me over in my career that I had to work my butt off to obtain.

"How are you going to arrest him if you don't know who he really is?" Quincey voices my own concern.

"I don't know yet. That's what I've been working on for the last eight hours rather than sleeping. But I will figure it out!" I declare because I'm a damn good agent when my brain isn't all foggy with need and longing for a sexy man I knew was too good to be true. "He's a damn good thief, so he probably has a criminal record."

"Great, so you just have to look through thousands of local mugshots," Quincey responds. "At least his face should jump right out at you since he's so freaking gorgeous."

"A *criminal* stole my laptop that is full of confidential government files because I was blinded by his good looks. How messed up is that?" I ask her. "I'm supposed to catch criminals, not get duped by them!"

"Have you tried contacting him again on the app?" she questions.

"His profile is long gone," I huff, since I tried that about half an hour after he left and didn't return my calls. I'm pretty sure he took his profile down before he even walked into the bar.

"Well, in a few hours, you can call the local pawnshops to see if he sold it," Quincey suggests.

"No. He wouldn't have pawned it. This whole scheme wasn't about money. He wore a nice, new suit and took the time to set up a fake dating profile and have business cards printed. He's more than a petty thief who stole for money. He's smart and patient." When it finally hits me, I exclaim, "Whoever he is, he must be after what's *on* the laptop!" The big picture starts to make more sense when I think about it from that angle. "Oh, god! What if he hacks into it and shares the files? Or reveals the names of confidential informants? I could lose my job if my superiors in Atlanta or...or the U.S. Attorney here finds out that I'm single-handedly responsible for blowing the lids off all of their investigations!"

"Then you need to figure out who *he* is, find him, and get the laptop back before anyone knows what happened!" she urges.

"I know!" I grumble. "First, I should probably go through the cases I've been working on and look at photos of all the suspects," I say as I think aloud. "Ugh! But it's kind of hard to do that when he has my damn laptop!"

"Calm down. You can use mine," she tells me, getting to her feet and retrieving it off the computer desk in the corner. "Did you save your work to our server?"

"Yes."

"Good, then you should be able to find everything," she says as she hands the laptop over.

Two hours and a giant pot of coffee later, we've been through all the files, along with hundreds of mugshots, yet we still have nothing.

"So, maybe you're wrong and he's not a suspect on a potential case," Quincey says with a sigh from her end of the sofa, where she's curled up with a blanket and pillow. Both of us called in sick today, since finding this asshole is worth missing a day of work.

"No, I don't think I'm wrong about that," I huff as I stretch my arms over my head, working out the stiffness. "If I had to guess, he's probably in one of the gangs, or associated with them, and they sent him to steal it because he *doesn't* have a record."

"That would be the smart criminal thing to do," Quincey agrees. "Who has the smartest gang?"

"Probably the one we don't have a shred of evidence on, even though they've been the number one suspects on shootouts, murders, *and* arsons in just the last year," I say, when it suddenly hits me. "Oh! And the same one that is located on the coast, which would fit with his stupid profile's claim that he likes, '*long walks on the beach*.'"

"Great! Who is that?" she asks.

"The Savage fucking Kings!" I shout.

It looks like I'm going be taking a trip out to the North Carolina coast to see about a handsome thief in a motorcycle gang.

CHAPTER THREE

Dalton

Heading to the chapel with my score, I walk in early with a few minutes to spare before our meeting starts. Most of the guys are already seated, each of them wearing the same identical Savage King MC leather cut as mine since the cuts are required for all meetings. The only time we take them off is when absolutely necessary, like going on a fake date with an ATF agent.

Last night, after I got back to my apartment, feeling a little off-balance and nauseous, I searched through Peyton's bag before I finally took off the fancy suit and fell asleep. There's a password of course on her computer, so I couldn't get in. But some of Peyton's notes were scribbled on a legal pad, along with her day planner and change purse that held twenty dollars and a few coins. If she had left any credit cards in there, I would've found a way to at least return those to her.

And for some reason, I spent more time than I should have reading every fucking thing I could find written in her neat, girly handwriting. She alternates going to yoga and spin class twice each week, which explains why she looks good enough to eat, literally. She recently got a haircut, and she's planning to go home for Thanksgiving, wherever her "home" is located. My guess is Atlanta.

"Here you go," I say to Reece when I place the leather briefcase down on the table and slide it to him. Then, remembering our stupid bet, I pull out a hundred-dollar bill from my wallet and toss it down. Sure, I could've snapped a photo of Peyton's panties around her ankles, but I didn't. I'd rather take the loss than have conned her out of anything else.

"Pleasure doing business with you," Reece says, reaching for the cash to slip it in the inside zipper of his cut. He's grinning like a kid on Christmas morning when he removes the laptop from the bag.

"You got it?" Chase asks as he watches Reece typing away on the keypad. "How the hell did you pull that off?"

"Carefully," I reply with a smirk.

"Okay, I'm in," Reece says a moment later when he somehow breaches Peyton's password in a matter of seconds. "Give me a few minutes?" he asks Torin, our president sitting like usual at the head of the table.

"Sure, brother," Torin answers, so Reece picks up the computer and heads down the hall to his apartment with it for some peace and quiet.

Turning his concerned gaze on me, Torin asks, "Do we have any blowback to worry about?"

"Nope."

"You're absolutely sure?" he asks me with one of his sandy-blond eyebrows raised suspiciously. "You just stole a laptop from the federal government. If you get caught, that shit is serious."

"Oh, I know," I say, my grin widening as I recall the incredibly erotic details of my heist. "Nothing to worry about. She won't report it."

"You better hope not," Abe huffs from across the table. "You're too pretty for federal prison. Wouldn't last a damn day."

"Ain't that the truth." I wink at him. "How long did your ugly mug last in prison? Years, right?" I ask, and the big man flips me off.

For about half an hour, we shoot the shit and discuss the MC's legitimate businesses and illegal side gigs that supplement our income. Since math is one of the few things I'm good at besides fighting and fucking, my job as the club's treasurer is to not only collect membership dues, but to sort out the best ways to funnel our dirty money into the legit enterprises before we send anything to our straight-as-an-arrow accountant. Keeping two sets of books isn't easy but someone has to do it, and Torin has enough shit on his plate trying to run the businesses.

Finally, Reece comes back with the report on his findings from the government's files.

"Good news," he says to the room as he stands in the doorway with Peyton's silver laptop still in his hands. "They don't have shit for evidence. The CI we ran off wouldn't tell them a damn thing other than our names, and it looks like they're just trying to connect the dots between us, the Aces, and the Cartel. The articles from the arson, bar shooting, and Cruz's death are all in there, but I didn't see anything that would tie that shit to us directly."

"Thank fuck," Torin mutters and we all heave a sigh of relief. "Now maybe we can get back to business as usual around here."

"Sounds good, boss," Reece says, along with the rest of our relieved words of agreements.

Although, I already know that forgetting the hot as fuck agent I screwed over is gonna be harder than I expected, especially since I can't seem to stop thinking about her, no matter how hard I try.

...

Peyton

"I'm here," I say into my cell phone after I circle the block and then park a few hundred feet away from the *Savage Asylum* parking lot that's known as the clubhouse for the Savage Kings MC.

"Are you sure this is a good idea? You should have let me come with you!" Quincey says into my ear. "These guys are dangerous, right?"

"I'm not stupid. I won't go running in with guns blazing," I tell her, with a roll of my eyes she can't see. "I'm just going to wait here and try to catch *Mr. Aycock* leaving alone." God, I should've known when he told me his last name was Aycock that he was a fraud. So childish.

"Keep me on the line until then," she says.

"Okay," I agree, since what I'm doing out here alone, staking out an MC gang, is not very smart. But desperate times call for desperate measures. I *have* to get that laptop back, preferably before they're able to crack my password.

How the asshole was able to so easily distract me, I'm not sure. Even when I was going through a messy divorce, I didn't make even a single minor error. Now this...

The worst part is that I was finally starting to regain enough confidence to start dating again, and after last night, I'm certain that it will be nearly impossible to believe anything that comes out of a man's mouth anytime in the near future.

It's one thing for a guy to use an old or misleading photo on his profile, but to pretend to be someone else entirely in order to steal from me? That level of betrayal blows my already apprehensive mind.

And makes me look like a complete fool.

Conducting background checks on potential suitors seemed a little extreme. Guess I was too naïve for my own good, and now that mistake is going to bite me in the ass. From here on out, I won't even meet another guy until I've learned and verified their full name and date of birth.

"So, what's the plan if you do see him?" Quincey asks in my ear.

"I'm just going to follow him and when I get him alone, I'll politely pull him over and ask him to give my computer back to me to avoid criminal charges," I say, like it's that simple.

"And if he refuses?"

"Let's hope that he doesn't," I mutter. Because if that happens, I'm fucked.

Before I left Raleigh on this insane mission, I put in a call to the CI who was trying to prospect for the MC before they figured out what he was up to a few weeks ago. The guy was evasive and shady, making it clear he wasn't thrilled about answering any of my questions. But I was finally able to get names for the two blond members. Once I added in the smirk and the fact that he could also make a living modeling underwear, he was able to narrow it down to just one name—Dalton Brady.

Based on the CI's intel during his few weeks prospecting, Mr. Brady is also an officer, the club's treasurer, probably involved with laundering all of the dirty money through the club's legit businesses, like the bar and strip club.

Surprisingly enough, Mr. Brady doesn't have a criminal record. In fact, other than his driver's license, there's nothing else on file for him, not even a single speeding ticket.

How is it that this guy can be a member of a motorcycle club that's caught up in so much violence it's scary and be so squeaky clean?

In addition to his good looks, he must be pretty damn smart.

That doesn't make me feel any better about how easily he was able to screw me over.

And don't even get me started on the hit to my self-esteem.

The whole time we were talking and then…later, when we were doing more, I thought he was actually attracted to me.

How could I have been so stupid?

Guys like him don't want women like me. They want beautiful, stick-thin, bikini models, not boring, plus-size federal agents with an overabundance of junk in the trunk.

So, not only am I pissed that he stole my laptop, but I'm also angry at the asshole for making me feel like an idiot.

Hopefully my threat of arresting him will be enough to get him to return my laptop. If he doesn't, I could lose my job. And that is just not something I'm willing to give up because of one jackass biker.

CHAPTER FOUR

Dalton

I spot the familiar black SUV sitting about five hundred feet down the street from the clubhouse's parking lot when I start to leave. So, it's no big surprise when I pull out and then look down in my mirror to see the vehicle following me.

Fuck.

So, I guess Peyton's already figured out who I am, and came to collect. The agent is really damn smart, I'll give her that. Did she come by herself or does she have a partner with her? If she's alone, then she's either insane or incredibly brave to confront me on her own.

Since I don't want any witnesses for this encounter, especially my MC brothers, who may get all worried and shit for no reason about an agent on my ass, I make a right turn off Highway 58 onto Canal Drive, a private wooded side road. Just as I expected, the blue light in her front dashboard comes on as soon as we're out of sight from the main highway.

I pull over onto the dirt shoulder slowly to stop and kill the engine. After I climb off my bike, I remove my helmet and hang it on one of the handlebars to turn around and see just how angry the hot little agent is with me.

She's even sexier than I remember from last night when she gets out and slams her door. Wearing a pristine white pant suit that I would love to get dirty, she struts up to me in her black heels with dark sunglasses covering her eyes. Her long blonde hair blows in front of her face, thanks to the coastal wind, which seems to piss her off even more when she has to bat it away.

"Good afternoon, Agent Bradley. What brings you to Emerald Isle on a such a lovely day?" I ask coolly with my patented smug grin.

"Cut the shit!" she shouts when she's right in front of my face. She grabs the collar of my t-shirt from the opening of my leather cut and balls it up in her fist. "Where the hell is my laptop?"

Smirking at her beautiful, angry face, I blink innocently and ask, "What laptop?"

She chokes me with my own shirt collar a little more and I have to say, rather than intimidate me, I'm just turned on by her show of force. Badass women may have just become my new fetish.

"Give it to me *now!*" she demands, which only makes my smile widen.

Cutting my eyes sharply to the left and then the right on the empty road, I say, "You drove all the way here just to finish what we started last night?" I reach for either sides of her hips to pull her body closer to mine while licking my lips, remembering exactly how damn good she tasted. One of my thumbs strokes over the metal badge clipped to her waistband while the other caresses her gun holster. "Okay, baby, I'm in. But, badge or not, if you keep flashing your pussy around town like a bitch in heat, you're gonna get both of us slapped with a public indecency charge."

I was fully expecting her knee to slam up and into my balls, but that doesn't mean it hurt any less.

"Motherfucker," I croak. When she pulls away from me, I double over in pain. Bracing a palm on the seat of the bike to keep myself upright, my other hand grabs my boys through the crotch of my jeans, trying to help them descend again.

During my recovery is when Peyton stomps around my bike to look in the saddlebag that's now empty. Coming back around, she pushes her sunglasses up to the top of her head to lean down and look at my face. That's the first time I notice how pronounced the bags are under her eyes. Again, that stupid fucking feeling of guilt squeezes its fingers around my throat.

"Last chance to turn over my laptop, *Dalton Brady,* before I take you in and charge you with theft of government property and...and assault on a federal employee," Peyton threatens me, but I know she's full of shit. If she wanted to have me arrested, she would need the U.S. Attorney to take charges against me to the Grand Jury, and then have *them* indict me. The feds only assemble a Grand Jury once a fucking month and if I had to guess, it wasn't today.

That's right, I'm smarter than I look.

If I wasn't in agony at the moment, I'd probably make another smartass comment, like I don't consider a consensual pussy-licking to be an assault, just to get her even more riled up.

But I keep my mouth shut.

And I have to say it's so fucking hot when she rough handles me. I don't even try to resist when she spins me around, jerks my hands behind my back, and slaps the metal handcuffs on my wrists. She then shoves me over toward her SUV and hustles me into the back-seat, right over the spot where she came for me not even twenty-four hours ago.

I'm not concerned about her little arrest. If I wanted to, I could run away, head back to the clubhouse, and have one of my brothers get the cuffs off. Instead, I'm curious to see just how far she's willing to take this charade of hers. The only thing I'm currently worried about is my baby sitting abandoned on the side of the road, with the key still in the ignition.

"Can I call someone...to come get my ride?" I ask Peyton through the subsiding nut pain after she flops down in the driver's seat.

"No," she answers, pulling her sunglasses back down over her eyes. "I hope it gets stolen!"

"That's just wrong," I tell her. "Did your laptop have sentimental value? I'm guessing it didn't. But you see that bike right there? It's a classic 1947 Harley Knucklehead. I helped my dad restore it before he..." I stop myself before I tell her my whole goddamn life story. "Look, it's fucking priceless, okay?" I huff. "The only material thing I give a shit about in this world is that damn bike."

Peyton freezes with her hands on the steering wheel at ten and two for several long, silent moments before she exhales, then thankfully, gets out to go and retrieve the key from the bike's ignition.

Back in the car, she throws the key ring at me, hitting me in the face with it before it falls between my legs since my hands are restrained behind me.

"Thank you," I tell her when she starts to drive away to who the hell knows where.

I begin to get an idea when she not only hits her turn signal to get on the highway headed west but makes a call to someone, simply saying, "I'm on my way back to Raleigh."

Shit.

So, either she's really taking me all the way back to Raleigh for questioning and holding until a warrant for arrest comes through, or this is all just one crazy, intense game of chicken. Since New Bern has the closest Eastern District of North Carolina federal building in our jurisdiction, not Raleigh, I'm gonna go with the chicken option.

"So, you're pretending like you're arresting me?" I ask Peyton as I scoot over toward the middle of the backseat until I can get a clear shot of her face in the rearview mirror, even though her sunglasses are hiding her eyes again.

She doesn't respond.

"Fine," I mutter. "Here, let me help you write up the arrest report." I get comfortable and rest my head back against the seat. Clearing my throat, I begin narrating our steamy meeting. "Late on the night of October sixth, the theft is believed to have occurred sometime between the half hour when the victim was face down in the backseat of her government-issued SUV, screaming through her orgasm in the Main Street parking garage. She alleges that only the *handsome* suspect was in the vicinity, but the wrongly accused suspect assures authorities that there were *plenty* of opportunities for the theft to occur since the suspect was so busy shoving his tongue in the victim's mouth and pussy that he was not aware of their surroundings..."

Peyton refuses to meet my gaze in the rearview during my narrative.

"Does that sound about right?" I ask.

"If it wasn't you, it was one of your gang buddies while I was... distracted," she huffs.

"Gang buddies? I don't have gang buddies. At least not anymore," I reply. "What I have are MC brothers. But they are upstanding gentlemen. None of them would *ever* steal from a federal agent while she was getting her pussy licked. That's just plain rude."

"So it was you," Peyton asks, her cheeks now a nice rosy red that I imagine is similar to the one she was probably sporting last night.

"I didn't say it was me. You just think it was me because I'm the easiest person to...finger for it," I say, unable to prevent my snicker.

"Just tell me where the damn laptop is!" she yells.

"If I *was* stupid enough to steal a federal agent's computer, I definitely wouldn't cop to it. Giving up a location would basically be admitting guilt, wouldn't it?"

"I have no idea why I *ever* found you attractive for even a second," she mumbles to herself.

"You wanted me so badly that it never occurred to you, with all of your higher education and law enforcement training, that I could be a thief. Now, you're mad at yourself for that lapse in judgment and you're taking it out on me, a completely innocent man."

"Either tell me where the laptop is, or I'll gag you, so you can't talk," she warns.

"Isn't it bad enough that you're kidnapping me?" I ask. "I mean, we both know that you're not taking me in and admitting what happened last night. If I had to guess, you already have a tough time making the men you work with take you seriously without adding the tongue-fucking in the public parking garage to your resume."

"Stop talking about that!" Peyton yells at me. "Believe me, I regret it. I'll regret that half hour for the rest of my life. I'm trying to forget it—you should too."

Her words sting, but I tell myself they're coming from a place of anger and not actual regret. She sure didn't sound like she was regretting anything at the time...

"That's not the whole truth, though, is it?" I question her since I was there, and she loved every second of what I did to her. "The problem is that you know you *won't* be able forget that the best sexual experience of your life was with an outlaw." When she doesn't answer, I go on to add, "And you can't help but wonder how good fucking would've felt if I hadn't walked away on you..."

"I'm gonna pull over and gag you," she threatens again.

"With what? Your tongue? You shoved it down my throat like you couldn't get enough..."

My words are cut off when she growls and then reaches to turn up the volume on the radio. "Sex Type Thing," the absolute last song I would expect to blast from her radio, erupts at ear-deafening levels from the speakers.

I'm sure that my laughter is still loud enough for her to hear before I shout, "Didn't peg you as a Stone Temple Pilot fan! You're just full of surprises, aren't you?"

CHAPTER FIVE

Peyton

What the hell am I doing?

That's the question that I've asked myself way too many times since last night in the bar.

I was blinded by one man's good looks and now I'm screwed. Not getting any sleep is wreaking havoc on my common sense.

But there are hundreds of confidential documents on my stolen laptop. In the wrong hands, someone could breach the entire federal network!

And while I wish it were as easy as taking the asshole in and having him locked up, I can't even begin to prove he took it. Sure, I could request the surveillance video from the parking garage, but only if I get a judge to sign off on a warrant, which means my superiors now and for the rest of my career going forward, would know that I fooled around with the suspect in our parking garage! If I admit to all of that, my career will be ruined. Not that it won't be if I can't get him to tell me where the hell he's hiding my laptop.

If I had to guess, it's probably back in the MC's clubhouse. I'm not stupid enough to try and go into the lion's den on my own, or in this case, the Savage Kings' den. We may not be able to prove that they've done anything illegal, but it's obvious that they're not just a bunch of good ole boy, motorcycle enthusiasts. The club president's pregnant wife was murdered in cold blood, so they no doubt enacted some sort of vengeance for that heinous crime. A normal man would kill for that, so I can only imagine the wrath of an MC gang leader who lost a loved one.

So, while I was happy that I was able to track down the bastard this morning and identify him leaving the clubhouse, now that he's handcuffed in the back of my car, I have no freakin' clue what I'm going do with him. And he won't shut the hell up!

Of all the songs that could've been on the satellite radio, why did the first one that came through the speakers have to be about the physical act I'm trying so hard to *not* think about?

The last thing I need is him throwing last night in my face over and over again. I feel stupid enough about it as it is. What I did was crazy and reckless, and I know better.

So why did I do it?

Because Henry, I mean *Dalton*, is ridiculously hot and irresistible.

At the time, I thought he was attracted to me too. But now I know that he was playing me all along, and I fell right into his trap.

My plan was to start driving in the direction of Raleigh and hope that he would panic, then confess before telling me to turn around so that he could return my property. Unfortunately, he didn't fall for my ploy.

I guess that means that my new plan is to hold him hostage and offer to exchange him for my laptop.

It's not the best idea, but it's all I have right now.

Besides, it's too late for me to do anything else.

I've already kidnapped him.

It feels like I'm sliding down an extremely slippery slope on my ass and I can't seem to stop myself.

Rather than make things better, I keep making them worse.

Dalton

"**G**et inside and don't think about trying anything," Peyton threatens when she stops the SUV in front of a row of nice, new townhouses and holds open the rear passenger door for me.

She brought me to her house? Why the hell would she do that? Guess she really is freaking out about my theft even more than I expected.

I hope that she's a more cautious agent than she is with strange men she meets on Tinder. If not, she's gonna find herself in all sorts of trouble. Why I give a shit about her safety, I'm not entirely sure.

"Can you put my bike keys in my pocket?" I ask, nodding to where they're still sitting on the seat.

With an annoyed huff, Peyton grabs the key ring and stuffs them in my front jean pocket. Then, she pulls her fucking gun on me, like that would stop me from overpowering her if I wanted, and motions for me to walk up the steps to her place.

Peyton unlocks the door and then shoves me inside with a push to my back. For some reason, she thinks she has all the power in this situation of ours because I'm restrained in her apartment. But actually, it's the opposite.

I have *all* of the power.

Only *I* know where her laptop is, and only *I* can give her that information. She can't go to the authorities now that she's illegally kidnapped me against my will. And if Peyton was suicidal enough to go marching into the clubhouse full of my brothers searching for it, she would have done so already.

I may as well be holding *her* hostage and have her tied up in my bed because she is well and truly fucked. Not that I would be opposed to Peyton restraining me in her bedroom...

"Take a seat and get comfortable," she says, pointing with the muzzle of the gun to the empty wall across the sparsely decorated living room. It's the spot that's furthest from the door.

My back slides down the wall and then I'm sitting with my knees up in front of me, shoulders starting to ache since my wrists are still restrained behind my back.

I did what she asked to make her think she has power over me. Now it's time to get to the fun part where I remind her who's really in charge here.

"Take off your shirt," I tell her once I'm as comfortable as I can get. I didn't get to see her titties last night, so I need to remedy that oversight now.

"What?" Peyton asks as she comes to a stop in front of me and lowers her gun so that it's now pointing down at the pristine ivory carpet. Who the hell has white carpet? More importantly, how does she keep it so clean?

"If you take off your shirt, then maybe I'll be able to recall a memory of what happened to your laptop," I explain to her.

She scoffs and rolls her eyes. "That is never going to happen, buddy."

"Then you're never gonna get your shit back," I respond. "And you and I both know that you can't keep me here forever..."

Her shoulders slump just a tad when the truth of that statement hits her.

"There has to be something else you want," she counters. "Do you want money? Give me back the laptop and I'll...I'll pay you five grand and let you go. We can call the payment a finder's fee."

I'm already shaking my head before she finishes her sentence. "Nope. Believe it or not, I have plenty of money. Do you know what I really want but don't have?" I ask, and then immediately give her the answer. "Titties."

Peyton barks out a non-humorous laugh. "You're out of your damn mind. Don't you think you've had enough fun at my expense when you humiliated me?"

"Fun at your expense? Humiliated you?" I repeat in confusion.

"Yes!" she exclaims, the indignation at what happened in the parking garage written all over her face. How dare she get pissed at me for having an orgasm when I got nada. And it was never my intention to embarrass her. I should've left after the kiss, but I didn't.

"Jesus, woman. Do you think it was fun for me to get you off with a rock-hard cock and then walk away without getting any relief for myself?" I ask.

"Poor pitiful you," she mutters sarcastically. "I'm *so* sorry you had to stoop so low to get what you wanted from me."

"I'm not sorry," I tell her. "The only thing I'm sorry about is that I had to meet you under false pretenses..."

"Ha! So you admit it then! You set me up to rob me!" Peyton shouts.

Shit. I almost said too much. Reel it in, Brady.

"The only thing I'm admitting to is wanting to fuck you," I contend. "That's all men on Tinder want, right? I set up a date just so I could try to fuck you. That was the false pretenses. But when my conscience caught up to me, I couldn't go through with it."

"Liar," she spits. "You are so full of shit. Men like you don't want women like me."

"It's the truth! The whole truth and nothing but the truth," I tell her. "Hook me up to a polygraph machine. The feds have them, right?" And what the hell did she mean when she said *men like me don't want women like her*? Criminals like me don't want to get their hands on hot, curvy, badass agents like her?

"Your MC is the only thing that's getting fucked," Peyton replies. "You busted our CI, he told you about my investigation, and you're trying to see how badly you're screwed."

"Too bad you don't have anything but circumstantial evidence," I mutter.

43

"That's what you think…"

"That's what I fucking know for a fact," I argue.

Peyton's eyes widen. "How would you know that?"

Grinning, I tell her, "Hypothetically, if the MC did get their hands on a government laptop, it would only take seconds for us to access files. Hypothetically, of course."

"Great," she grumbles, reaching up to run her fingers through her hair while her other hand still holds the gun by her thigh. "That's just great. Criminals stole my computer and accessed confidential files. I have to report this shit to my superiors, and then I'll be screwed…"

"You want it back?" I ask her, interrupting her worried rambling. I don't want her to lose her damn job for this. The MC got what we needed from it, so there's no reason we can't return it. "You can have the laptop back. No one has to know that it was temporarily missing."

"I've been asking you for it for hours!" Peyton exclaims.

"Right," I say. "And I'm agreeing to return the laptop right into your hands. There's only one thing you have to do."

"What?" she asks, brow furrowed because she's already forgotten my request.

"Take off your shirt."

"Oh my god!" she huffs. "We are *not* going back to that nonsense."

"Then I guess we're right back to where we started—you kidnapping me against my will and me refusing to tell you anything about your missing computer."

Peyton mutters something under her breath, but then she places the gun down on the floor and starts to unbutton the top of her white shirt.

Holy shit, she's actually gonna do it.

My mouth waters as the first hints of her white lacy bra and hidden skin appear through the opening of her blouse. Before she even gets her arms free, I add, "Bra too. Seeing bare tits *really* helps me to remember things."

"No," she replies without even considering it.

"Yes," I counter forcefully, leaving no room for argument, reminding her this isn't a negotiation.

After her shirt is in a pile on the floor, we have a staring contest that lasts for about two minutes before she eventually caves.

"You're a foul, perverted asshole," she grumbles while reaching behind her back to unhook her bra, letting the straps fall down her arms before tossing it to the carpet. "There! Now get me my damn laptop so I can let you go!"

"The shirt and bra stay off until it gets here," I demand as my eyes take in all of the creamy skin of her beautiful breasts and perky pink nipples. "Oh, and you have to stop investigating the Savage Kings."

"You know I can't do that."

If I could lift my gaze to her face, I bet it would show pure outrage.

"Then I guess you'll never see your laptop again," I mutter. "Such a shame for you to lose your job once the feds find out you gave away all their secrets for a tongue lashing. Do you think they'll arrest you when they find out about the kidnapping?"

I do look up in time to see her roll her eyes again and blow out a breath that flutters the strand of blonde hair out of her face. "Fine. I'll lay off the Kings as long as they don't become suspects in any new crimes."

"Great! Pull my phone out of my pocket." The burner phone is in the back-right jean pocket, but I don't tell her that when she comes over and kneels in front of me, her heavy tits swaying in front of my face close enough to lick. I let her dig into each front pocket, pulling out my personal phone first.

"Nope. Not that one," I tell her.

"You have two phones?" Peyton looks up at my face to ask me through her thick, black eyelashes. We're so close that, for the first time, I can clearly see how stunning her hazel eyes are, with various shades of green swirls circling the pupil. There are an infinite number of rings and I want to count them all.

"Yeah," I answer her question once I get to six circles of green and am finally able to break free from the distracting spell her eyes put me under.

"Of course you do," she mutters when she stuffs the device back in the pocket, like she's annoyed I'm a criminal with two phones. Or maybe the notion holds some other meaning I don't understand.

Eventually, Peyton removes the burner phone from my right back pocket with an annoyed huff.

"Find Reece's name in my contacts, call him, and then hold it up to my ear," I instruct, and her beautiful eyes narrow at me, making me think she isn't fond of following someone else's orders.

Her fingers get to work, though, and a moment later, the device is ringing next to my ear while she holds it to my head. I think I could drown in her sweet peachy scent with her tits hanging in my face and die a happy man, right here and now.

"Yeah?" Reece answers.

"Hey, man. Can you have Eddie go load up my bike from Canal Drive?" I ask, first and foremost, making Peyton sigh heavily.

"Oh-kay," he agrees, as if wondering why I didn't call Eddie directly.

"And then could you give the laptop to the prospect and have him bring it to me?"

Reece laughs into the phone with understanding, before he says, "Are you up shit creek without a paddle?"

"Not entirely," I mutter, wetting my lips and eyeing Peyton's tits. Fuck, I want to put one of her pink nipples in my mouth.

"Let me guess. You're at her place in Raleigh?" he asks, having already figured out my situation.

"Yep."

"Shit. I thought that SUV parked outside this morning looked familiar. You good? Need any backup?"

"Nope, I am fan-fucking-tastic," I assure him honestly, since my only complaint at the moment is that my hands are restrained behind my back.

"Then sit tight. I'll send the kid off right now," Reece says before he ends the call.

"It's on the way," I tell Peyton.

"Good," she says as she closes the phone and straightens in front of me. Tossing the phone down next to me on the floor, her hands go to her hips. "Wait. You didn't tell him my address."

"Didn't have to," I respond with a wink. "You're not the only one who's been doing some investigating."

"Now I really should arrest you," she grumbles before walking a few feet away and taking her breasts out of my line of sight.

"Hey, you're the one who kidnapped me and brought me to your house!" I remind her. "You shouldn't have showed me where you live unless you planned to kill me. It's a rookie mistake." I withhold the fact that I sat out front with Reece and watched her for two days last week.

"Do you ever stop talking?" Peyton asks when she turns to face me again.

"Yes. Whenever there's something in my mouth. A tongue would suffice. Or a titty. I'm pretty fond of pussy, especially yours..."

Going over to her discarded clothes, Peyton picks up her shirt, strolls over, and then crouches down to press the fabric to my mouth, typing the ends at the back of my head. Which is fine because her tits are pressed against my face again while she works.

"I agreed to remain topless, but I didn't agree to stand in front of you." Then, she smiles smugly at me before she picks up her gun and walks away with a proud sway of her hips, down a hallway.

Really? Did she forget I'm not restrained to the floor, that I can get up and move around? It only takes a second to get to my feet, then wiggle the shirt out of my mouth so it falls down to my neck, and eventually flutters to the floor when it comes untied.

Tiptoeing as much a man who is well over six feet tall and weighs two-hundred plus pounds can, I ease down the hall until I locate her bedroom. It's empty but the door inside of it is shut. She must be in the bathroom, so I go over and stretch out on her bed, my booted feet spread eagle, cuffed hands behind my back, lifting the crotch of my jeans up in offering.

The bathroom door opens and then Peyton gasps before yelling, "What are you doing in here?" She even pulls out her gun from her pants holster to point it at me.

"You didn't tie me down to anything," I remind her.

"Get back in the living room!"

"We have a few hours before the laptop gets here. Want to have some fun?" I ask, thrusting my hips in the air. "You could start with blowing me as a thank you for the tongue fucking I gave you last night."

"Sure," she says sweetly with a sardonic smile. "If you want me to bite your dick off."

"Once you see my masterpiece cock, you won't want to hurt it," I tell her. "It's too fucking incredible to destroy."

"Get up and get back to the living room," she orders with her arm and gun pointing the way.

"I could've fucked you last night," I remind her. "You would've let me, and you would've loved it. But I didn't."

"Oh, you fucked me all right," she mutters, lowering her arm to cross both over her chest, gun still in her grip. "Just not in an enjoyable way."

"Now, that's not exactly true," I tell her. "You creamed on my face so hard that your juices were dripping down my chin."

"Stop talking about that!" Peyton snaps. She raises the gun this time when she says, "Go."

"Can I at least sit on the sofa?" I ask as I squirm over to the side of the bed and get to my feet.

"Fine," she huffs. "Just get out of my bedroom and don't say another word!"

Wow. She's really pissed because she wants me, and she's just too angry at me to give in and touch me.

48

But I have a feeling it won't take much for me to get Peyton out of her panties again.

In fact, I bet after she gets her laptop back, she'll be much more likely to get naked with me. She's halfway there already since she's topless.

Besides, it's true what they say. Angry sex is in fact one of the best kinds of sex. And right now, I'm pretty sure Peyton is so furious with me, she would fuck my brains out.

CHAPTER SIX

Peyton

When the doorbell rings about two hours later, I glare at the jackass lounging on my white sofa like a king and then shove my gun into the holster on my pants. Quickly slipping on my shirt, sans bra, I button it up on the way to answer the door.

A glance out the peephole shows a young kid in a leather vest similar to the one all of the Kings wear. Dalton referred to him on the phone as a prospect, so he's nothing more than an errand boy for the club. Still, I take in his baby face and red hair, dark eyes, remembering every detail so I can try and add him to the file later.

"Open it," Dalton says from the sofa because he obviously thinks I'm nervous and that's why I'm taking my sweet time. "He's a kid. He won't hurt you."

As opposed to himself, a big, grown-ass man who has a twinkle in his gorgeous blue eyes that make it obvious he likes hurting people. He sure as hell hurt me. Maybe not physically, but he lied to me and used me to steal my shit. Then I let him manipulate me into going topless for hours. He really is too pretty and smart for his own good.

Too bad I was lying about laying off the Savage Kings investigation. Now, I won't stop until every single one of the bastards wearing the bearded skull crown goes down.

Unlocking the deadbolt, I pull open the door and snatch my briefcase from the boy's hands before he even knows what happened. Then I shut the door back in his face and lock it.

"There. You got it," Dalton calls out from the sofa. "Now get these fucking cuffs off of me!"

"Hold on," I tell him while I take the bag over to the small kitchen table and set it down to pull out the laptop and start it up. Once I enter in my password, it loads my home screen, and everything looks intact. I click on a few files, the Savage Kings one first, to make sure nothing has been erased. Seems like it's all there, which is a huge freakin' relief.

"Happy now?" Dalton asks from right behind me, making me jump about a foot off the floor.

"Jeez," I mutter.

Why do I keep forgetting he's not bolted down to anything? He sure does know how to sit still and make people forget how dangerous he is. Last night, the idea he was a biker who came to the white-collar bar posing as an attorney, with the intention of robbing me, never crossed my mind.

Facing him once I get my heart rate down, I pull out the small handcuff key from my pants pocket and tell him, "Turn around." He does, giving me his back that's covered in the huge Savage Kings patches, including the smug bearded skull wearing a crown. They call themselves Kings, like they think they're untouchable. We'll just see about that.

Finally, I turn the metal in the lock so it clicks open, and remove the cuffs from each of the jerk's wrists.

"That's much better," Dalton says when he turns around and looks down at me with those too-gorgeous-to-be-real blue eyes while his fingers massage his wrists. "I'm all for getting handcuffed, but it would be a helluva lot more fun if we were in bed and naked."

"Get out," I tell him, pushing aside any thoughts of him and me naked from my mind, despite how intriguing the stupid idea may seem at the moment.

"No," he replies.

"No?" I repeat with an unfiltered gasp of surprise. "The cuffs are off. You can go now," I say. "If you hurry, I bet you can catch a ride back with your friend."

"He can leave without me. I'm not ready to go just yet," Dalton tells me with his gaze lowered to my lips.

Oh no. No way am I falling for his crap again! And dammit, why am I shaking? I'm not scared of him. If he wanted to hurt me, I know the cuffs wouldn't have stopped him.

"Do I need to show you where the door is?" I ask, hoping he can't hear the new shakiness in my voice.

"Nope. I remember," Dalton says, then takes the handcuff keys from my hands and puts them on the kitchen table beside my laptop. "And if you really wanted me gone, you would've pulled your gun on me again."

"I-I do want you gone," I contend, but I'm not even sure if I believe the words. My back is against the chair at the table with his big body looming over me. I should slip out from between the tight space or shove him back a few feet. Yes, that's exactly what I'm going to do.

But when I flatten my palms on his stomach that's so hard and defined I can feel the contours of his washboard abs through two layers of his clothing, they don't do what my brain instructed them to do. It's not their fault for getting the message confused while touching not just any man but one built to perfection.

"So, what's it going to be, Peyton? Should I stay, or should I go?" he asks, weakening my knees with the use of my name.

Gathering my nerve, I glance up at Dalton's handsome face. He lifts a single blond eyebrow at me and says, "Want me to answer that question for you?"

"No false pretenses or...or thefts this time?" I question him.

"All I want to take is your breath away when I'm buried deep inside of you," he replies, which is the perfect response to snap the last shred of my hesitancy. Possibly my dignity too, but at the moment, the only thing I want is for him to fulfil that exact goal.

Grabbing one of my hands from his stomach, Dalton guides it lower to the hard bulge in the front of his jeans and says, "If you need proof that I wasn't lying last night or right now about wanting you, here it is. You remember rubbing up on him, don't you? He sure as fuck remembers you. There's no faking a hard cock."

God yes, I remember. How could I forget?

"Now answer my question, Peyton," he demands, using his grip on the top of my hand to squeeze his shaft.

"Stay," I say so softly I'm not even sure if Dalton heard. But before I can speak the single word again, his mouth is crashing down on mine, his tongue forcing its way past the seam of my lips to get to my own. The unexpected kiss is as hot and fierce as the one last night, demanding my full attention.

Dalton's rough hands tightly grasp the sides of my waist then move up to cup my breasts through my shirt. Each of his hands grip the opposite sides of the fabric and jerk, ripping the material apart down the middle and sending buttons flying through the air.

He attacks me like...like a savage right there in the middle of my kitchen! And it's so hot, I nearly combust.

The next thing I know, my suit pants are ripping at the zipper seam and then those magical fingers of his are plunging down the front my panties, searching, possessing, owning me.

"I hate you," I murmur against his lips while shoving the leather cut off his shoulders, in a hurry to get him undressed.

Pulling back to look at me with a smirk, his fingers never missing a single thrust in and out of my panties, Dalton asks, "Why? Because you went for a ride on my tongue and it felt so good you never want to get off?"

"Yes," I answer on a gasp when he strokes that powder keg inside of me so damn good.

"Just wait until your pussy gets a taste of my cock," he says as his lips, tongue, and teeth come down to devour my neck. "You'll spend the rest of your life on your back with your legs spread, begging me to come inside of you again."

I don't doubt his arrogance one bit, not after how much he made me feel in so little time last night. That's why I want him so badly. I know sex with Dalton will be incredible. At the moment, I really wish someone, anyone other than the smug thief could turn my world upside down, but it looks like I'm stuck with him.

I finally manage to get his t-shirt over his head and then my palms are splayed on his smooth, bare chest. My hands soak up the warmth of his skin while I inhale his masculine cologne and leather scent as I caress his defined pecs. Moving down, I count an eight, not six, pack of rolling abs.

It's not fair. He's too damn hot to resist.

"Oh, god," I moan, having to grip his shoulders to hold myself up when his fingers become the best and worst thing that have ever happened to me. He plays me like a musical instrument he mastered a long time ago.

Dalton's arm goes around my back to pull me flush against his hard body when my thighs tense.

"Ohhh," I groan through the trembling waves of pleasure before I bite down on the sexy man's shoulder to see if his body is as delicious as he looks. And it is. Dalton's salty skin makes me think of something else on his body I wouldn't mind putting in my mouth. Once I get a taste of him, it's like I can't stop. I lick and suck my way up his neck then shove my fingers through his messy blond hair to tilt it to the side to keep at it.

"Fuck, you're a ferocious little sex kitten when you're horny," Dalton mutters.

"Shut up and take off your pants," I tell him since mine are already around my knees.

"Pants? Where we're going, we don't need...pants," he says in what I'm guessing is a horrible imitation of Doc from *Back to the Future*. It's so bad it almost makes me put the brakes on this whole scene. *Almost.*

"Oh, my god. Do you ever stop running your mouth?" I pull back to look up at him while still gripping his stupid, soft, and perfect hair.

His hands work diligently on getting his belt undone and then it's just a matter of popping a button and lowering the zipper on his jeans. Once that's taken care of, he grabs my chin between his fingers and says, "I want to fuck this angry little mouth of yours so damn much. But I'm afraid you really might bite my dick off after the way you were chomping down on my neck."

When I start to give him an indignant response, the jerk slams my jaw closed again.

"No, this time I'm gonna eat your pussy inside out instead," he says, using his free hand to jerk my panties down my legs. "Bet you won't have any more complaints about my mouth when you're coming on my face again."

Before I can finish taking a breath to respond, Dalton is on his knees with his nose and mouth pressed between my legs, stroking his hot, wet tongue back and forth rapidly over my clit before he wiggles the entire thing right up inside of me.

"Holy shit!" I exclaim, clutching at his shoulders to keep myself upright. My eyes roll back in my head and then I give myself over to the foul thief. He could do anything he wants to me right now and I would gladly let him.

Dalton gives me two earth-shattering orgasms, one right after another, with his tongue, while his hand dives into his open jeans and starts stroking his shaft. It's so hot, watching him jerk off, that I come again before he pulls his mouth off of me and gets to his feet.

He pulls off his shoes to remove his jeans all the way, leaving him standing completely naked in front of me. Reaching into a pocket of his pants still in his hand, Dalton retrieves a foil wrapper and then tosses the denim aside. He opens the condom with trembling hands like he's so turned on he can't control himself.

"Hurry up," I tell him while I strip all the way out of the rest of my clothes.

The jackass lifts a single menacing blond eyebrow at me before he stalks toward me like I'm about to pay for that demand. All the while, his right hand is stroking his condom-covered shaft, making it impossible to look away.

"You like bossing people around, telling them what to do, don't you?" he asks, just as he reaches around to grab both of my ass cheeks and haul me up his spectacular hard body as if I weigh nothing. I wind my arms around his neck and legs around his waist, too busy wiggling against his hard cock that's nestled between our bodies to worry about being too heavy for him to hold.

"But when we're fucking, *I'm* the one who calls the shots," he growls before his teeth nip at my neck. "I'll give you my cock when I damn well please, woman. First, I want you to beg me for it."

Scoffing, I tell him, "I'm not begging you for anything."

Lifting my ass up higher, demonstrating just how strong he is, he impales me on just the crown of his cock, making me gasp at the invasion. He's so thick and perfect and I need more. But the jackass holds me in place with a show of immense strength, refusing to give me another inch.

"Keep squirming. If you want more, you have to say the magic words," he tells me, trying to sound tough, even though his jaw is ticking and there's sweat beading on his forehead. He needs more just as much as I do, and if he doesn't put me down soon, he may drop me.

"Fuck you," I huff.

"Not yet."

He pulls me completely off of his cock and then lowers me, so that my slit strokes all the way up and down the outside of his length, and more importantly, his hard shaft presses on my clit. My hips dip to try and take him inside of me. Of course, the jerk won't allow that, though.

"Say it," he demands through gritted teeth.

"Fuck me," I tell him, but he only keeps up the teasing until my head falls back on a moan. "Oh god. Please...please, fuck me," I moan, saying the words before I can even stop myself. My head pops back up and my eyes widen as I look at him in shock.

"I knew you would break," the bastard says with a smirk. Then he lowers me all the way down on his cock until I bottom out.

"Dalton!" I cry out on a gasp.

Before I have time to adjust to his immense size, he slams my back against the closest wall, invading me so deeply I'm not sure if I'll ever be able to forget he was there. I'm so unbelievably full that I can't breathe, and that's probably why it takes me several minutes to realize my fingernails are digging violently into Dalton's back. He doesn't seem to mind, his thoughts and movements forceful and urgent, like they've been flipped to autopilot, focused on the primal urge to pump his hips, driving me literally up the wall.

"Yes, yes, yes!" I scream with each and every hard thrust as I slam my eyes shut to chase yet another orgasm. I need it so bad that my lower belly cramps. "Harder!" I demand, whimpering when the pressure inside me builds and builds. I'm so close I can almost touch the pleasure, if he would just pick up the pace!

"Fuck!" Dalton shouts when he pounds me into the wall one last time, his steely length finally hitting the perfect spot to set off the fireworks behind my closed eyelids. My inner walls spasm around his shaft at the exact same moment he swells, and I feel his hot, pulsing release, even through the condom.

It is hands down the best sex of my life. There's not even a close second with my ex, or anyone else I ever dated. Knowing it was with an outlaw sobers me up pretty fast, even though the happy tingly ruminants of repeatedly orgasming continue to flood the majority of my body and mind.

"I-I..." I try to speak, but there's not enough air in my still recovering lungs.

"What, what is it?" Dalton asks from where his face is buried in my neck while he pants heavily, blowing his warm breath over my skin.

"I want to hate you," I tell him. "But it's hard, after that."

"I want to hate you too. I think you made my back bleed," he says with a deep chuckle that makes his softening cock twitch inside of me. "But I sure do love your pussy."

When he pushes away from the wall, with me still hoisted in his arms, I ask, "What do you think you're doing?"

"I'm taking you to bed," he replies simply as he starts down the hallway. "I'm not leaving until we do that a few more times."

CHAPTER SEVEN

Dalton

I love sex just as much as the next guy.

And while I can easily go all night, I usually get my fill with the club sluts after a quick blowjob and standard doggy style fuck before I thank them and send them on their way. The girls get the job done, but I have the feeling they enjoy the sex more than I do.

Over the years, getting laid at the clubhouse has become so routine that the names and faces of the girls barely even register. Each night is like every other—they go down on me then get on their hands and knees. It's like living in a factory of cookie-cutter fucks. It's easy and convenient, sure, just never all that exciting.

"God, yes! Fuck me harder. Yes, harder, jackass! Fuck me...fuck me like an animal!"

See, that's not a phrase I'm used to hearing during sexy time. So, when Peyton is facedown, ass up on her bed, telling me how she wants me to do her, I can't wait to fulfill her request.

Grabbing both of her wrists, I pin her arms to her lower back with one of my hands while shoving my cock into her deeper, harder, faster until she's no longer capable of saying words, only incoherent cries and animalistic sounds.

"Is this how you wanted it last night in the parking garage?" I ask her when my other hand jerks on her blonde hair and wraps it tightly around my fist, so that I'm now controlling every inch of her beautiful, curvy body.

"*Yea-yesss!*" she exclaims between the wet slapping sounds of our bodies colliding. She's so turned on. And for once in my life, I would love to ditch the condom, so I can feel her hot, slippery flesh tightening around my thrusting cock.

"I'm coming! I'm coming!" she shouts, like the pleasure is taking her by surprise, before her pussy clamps down on me so hard my entire body shudders.

Fuck, it's good. I pound into her through the spasms until I can't hold off even a second longer.

"Wow," Peyton mutters into the pillow her face is burrowed in. "I've never got off during..."

"Seriously?" I ask before I pull out and throw myself down on the mattress beside her, too exhausted to even take care of the condom right this second.

"Yeah," she answers from where she's stretched out on her stomach, arms clutching the pillow under her head with her face turned toward me. "I'm sure those two times were just a fluke, though. There's no way you could pull off a hat trick." The corners of her lips lift into a taunting smirk.

Giving her ass a swift slap with my palm that makes her yelp, I tell her, "Wanna bet? Roll over so that I can prove you wrong."

And I do, over and over again, until the last round when Peyton is riding my cock. She gets off the final time with a shout of my name before she falls forward on my chest.

"Peyton?" I ask after a few minutes when she doesn't move or make a sound. She doesn't give a response, having passed out with me still buried inside of her.

I don't mind. Especially when the sweat on my skin starts to cool. It's like I have a Peyton blanket on me. And she smells so damn good too, like me and peaches all mixed together. I press my nose into her hair where the scent is the strongest, imagining her naked and sudsy, alone in her shower with her face tilted up, running her fingers through her long, damp locks. If I were capable of getting hard again, I'm certain I would just at the image of water cascading down her tits and the nice, round swell of her ass.

The only thing that would make that fantasy even better is if I were in her shower too, pressing the front of her body into the shower wall while fucking her from behind and...washing her hair with peach shampoo?

Jesus. I think Peyton really did fuck my brains out because I have never gotten turned on thinking about shampoo before. I'm starting to worry that from now on, just coming into contact with a can of peaches might make my dick hard.

How is that possible after one damn night?

Well, two, if you count making out with her yesterday in the parking garage. She smelled delicious then too, but it wasn't as nice and strong as it is here, lying in her bed.

For hours, I lay there awake, underneath her while she sleeps on top of me, stroking her hair and the soft skin of her back. It's the most non-sexual contact I think I've ever had with another person, and it's...really nice.

And exactly why I never let women linger around after we screw.

I don't need or want to think about them as anything but a good time, and it's hard to do that when they become warm, cozy Peyton blankets for hours.

I'm sure it's just all the endorphins she got flowing through me that's making me want to cling to her for as long as I can.

While I was pretty sure I could get Peyton naked, I had no idea how damn good the sex would be. She seemed timid and self-conscious when we met at the bar, but once she got angry and wound up, she turned into a little sex kitten.

The woman dug her claws in me, literally, and gave me a night I know I won't ever be able to forget, no matter how hard I try.

As crazy as it sounds, I already want to see her again, and I haven't even left yet.

The question is, will Peyton want to see me again? I guess that depends on whether or not she wakes up as the uptight agent or the feisty sex kitten.

Trying to figure out how to make sure it's the latter is what keeps me up for a few more hours...until Peyton eventually squirms off of me in her sleep, leaving me cold and feeling empty. Too bad I couldn't keep her there all night.

But maybe there *is* a way to make her stay in bed with me in the morning...

Peyton

I wake up with my arms stretched out over my head and a tongue between my legs. My thighs fall open wider with my full permission and approval, even though the muscles are all tight from one hell of a workout last night.

"God, I love it when you do that," I moan as my back arches and I blink my eyes open to watch Dalton's talented mouth fuck me. He lifts his face just long enough to flash me a grin and say, "Pussy—the breakfast of champions," before he gets back to work.

I want to reach down and run my fingers through his messy, sexy blond hair that looks like a halo on the Angel of Orgasms in the morning light...but I can't pull my arms down.

"What the—" I ask, as I twist my neck around to see the handcuffs hanging from one of the slits in the top of the headboard.

I hear and feel the vibration of Dalton's chuckles when he realizes I've finally figured out he restrained me in my sleep.

"Next time you use them on me, I better at least get a blowjob out of it," he tells me. My thoughts are still circling back to the phrase *next time* when the tip of his tongue circles my clit and his finger plunges in and out of me until nothing else in the world matters.

"*Yes! Yes! AHHH!*" I scream as my release ripples through my body and shakes me to my core.

"Damn, your pussy is so juicy and sweet," Dalton says as he kisses his way up my body, giving each of my nipples a morning tongue bath before he sits up on the side of the bed naked...to start getting dressed. He stands up and pulls on his jeans, which gives me a good view of the red streaks running through his Savage Kings tattoos on his back. "Well, it's been fun, but I've got to run."

"Good," I say, since I never intended for him to sleep over.

Or for me to sleep with him.

Several wonderful times.

Hold on. He's not really leaving right this second, is he? While I'm still handcuffed?

Next, from the pile of clothes he must have rounded up earlier from the kitchen, his white t-shirt goes on, then his shoes and socks. Finally, his black leather MC cut.

"Dalton?" I ask while jerking on the handcuffs.

"Oh, right!" he says with a slap of his palm to his forehead. "I left the key for you."

"Where? Where's the key?" I ask, starting to grow more concerned.

Licking his lips with a grin, he rests one knee on the bed to lean over and place a soft kiss on my neatly-groomed mound. With a wink, he straightens and looks down at me. "Wish I could stay and see how you Houdini them out."

"Oh, screw you," I huff.

"You want me again so soon?" he asks on his way toward the bedroom door.

"Unlock the damn cuffs!" I shout.

He ignores me.

"Are you kidding me? Dalton!"

"See ya, kitten," he says as he looks over his shoulder to leer at my naked body for a few more seconds before he walks out of the room.

"Damn you!" I yell, while I continue to flail with no improvement. "Go to hell, you asshole!"

"Funny, that's exactly where my mother says I'm headed!" he calls back from inside the apartment before I hear the front door open.

"*I hate you!*" I screech at the top of my lungs, so loud that the neighbors probably hear.

"Love you too!" his smug voice yells back before the front door closes.

My chest tightens while I lie still and silent, listening, waiting. He's gonna come back, right? I mean, he has to. He can't leave me like this. It's physically impossible for me to pull a key from my cunt and unlock the cuffs with my hands above my head!

Several more minutes pass as I listen to my panting breath and racing heart.

Oh, god.

He's not coming back.

He's an outlaw biker. Why would I think he gives a shit about how long I lie here before someone finds me?

That's when an embarrassingly loud sob breaks free, deafening in the otherwise silent bedroom.

...

Dalton

I am such a dick.

    I mean, yeah, I already knew that, but I'm taking dick to a whole new level.

Just thinking about Peyton's sexy body squirming, trying to get to that key that doesn't exist is making me hard. I make it five steps down the sidewalk before I turn around and have to stop myself from going back.

No. No! We need food first. And some rehydration. I mean, a man can only screw so many times in a night without refueling before his body starts to give out.

Hopefully after some breakfast and OJ, we can get back down to it.

Since I don't have a car because, hello, I was kidnapped, I walk on foot to the closest restaurant – a mom and pop country cooking joint that smells delicious. At the counter, I order two of everything they're serving: eggs, ham, bacon, toast, pancakes, a few muffins, and some fruit with the juice to go.

After the waitress walks away, I glance around and notice that everyone in the place is staring at me. While I never know if it's my looks or my cut that draws most eyes, today I'm guessing it's the goofy ass grin on my face, thinking about the naked woman I have tied up back in her bedroom.

"'Sup?" I ask the three old women at the closest booth. "Beautiful morning, isn't it?"

They giggle and look away after that, leaving me alone with my thoughts.

My cell phone chooses that moment to ring, so I pull it out and answer it. "Yeah?"

"Where the hell are you?" Reece asks.

"In Raleigh. Why?" I ask. "Something up?"

"When you didn't come home last night, or answer your phone the five times I called, I thought for sure you had been arrested! I checked all the jails in the five counties from here to Wake and didn't see you on any of the rosters."

"Nope, not in jail, obviously, if I'm answering my phone," I reply with a roll of my eyes he can't see. "But I could use a ride. Can you have the prospect come pick me up in the van?"

"Why didn't you just ride back with him yesterday?" Reece huffs.

"Because I wasn't ready to leave yet," I respond.

"Same address?" he asks.

"Yep."

Reece mutters a curse. "I'll send him on his way." He heaves an annoyed sigh before hanging up on me. That dude really needs to get laid. He's way too high-strung.

Finally, after a short, maybe fifteen-minute wait, my to-go order is bagged, ready, and paid for, so I'm on my way back to Peyton's apartment.

I hear her sobs before I even turn the doorknob in my hand and the sound is more painful than the bloody claw marks she left down my back.

Fuck.

Inside the apartment, I drop the bag of food on the kitchen table and rush to the bedroom.

Peyton's crying. She's curled up in a ball on her side, as much as she can with her arms still handcuffed to the headboard.

"Shh. It's okay," I tell her as I reach for her wet face.

"No! Don't touch me!" she yells, making my hand lower instantly.

"Peyton, I'm sorry," I say over her weeping. "I was coming right back. Did you really think I would leave you here like this?"

I reach over on the nightstand and grab the keys, glad I didn't actually leave them inside of her. She didn't see them? They were right beside her!

A second later, and I have the cuffs clicking open. Peyton wraps her arms around her knees that are drawn up to her chest while she continues to sniffle.

"Hey, it's okay," I tell her and place a hand on her shoulder.

"Don't touch me, you son of a bitch!" she yells before she jolts into a sitting position and starts swinging her fists at me. Hard. Unlike most women, she actually can pack one hell of a punch.

"Jesus!" I exclaim, while trying to block her blows and capture her wrists to make her stop.

After several minutes, she finally tires out or gives up, and starts to collapse back on the mattress before I scoop her up in my arms.

I tense up, expecting her to fight me again but she doesn't. She lets me hold her.

"I'm sorry," I tell her as she buries her face against my shirt and I listen to her soft sniffles. "I'm so sorry. I thought you knew I'd be right back. You really do think I'm an asshole."

She trusted me enough to sleep with me, and then she thought I went and screwed her over. Again. But that wasn't my intention. Hell, I know damn well what it's like for someone to have all the power over you and abuse it. That shit leaves scars. Which is why I haven't let myself get to know a single woman since I got brutally fucked over when I was a stupid, naïve teenager. Eight years is a long time to carry a grudge with the opposite sex, all because of one woman, yet I haven't been able to let it go and trust that I won't get used up all over again.

But I wasn't trying to hurt Peyton when I handcuffed her this morning. In fact, I thought she would laugh once I came back with breakfast and told her the key was right beside her the whole time.

She lets me hold her until her crying eventually stops and the sniffles die down.

"You had me cuffed a lot longer yesterday," I remind her.

"You-you're evil. I didn't...leave you...restrained to anything," she hiccups.

"Do you want to now?" I offer.

"No," she answers as she lifts her head and swipes her hand under each eye.

"You hungry? I brought breakfast," I tell her.

"I think I'll just, um, get a shower."

"Yeah, okay," I reply, wishing I could join her but know that now is not the time to ask.

When she tries to slip out of my lap, I kiss her cheek before I finally let go, surprising both her and myself. We freeze at the sweet and unexpected gesture before she gets to her feet and hustles on wobbly legs to the bathroom.

Peyton showers for a long damn time.

So long, in fact, I'm pretty sure she's hoping I'll give up and leave. But I'm not because I don't want to go until I know she's okay. My ass sits right there in the kitchen chair and doesn't move.

Besides, I still have another hour or so before my ride shows up.

Finally, I hear the door in her bedroom open and then her soft footsteps as Peyton heads toward the kitchen, right to the place where we first fucked yesterday.

"This is a lot of food," she says when her feet come to a stop at the head of the table. Her blonde hair is still damp but pulled up on top of her head, and she's wearing a fluffy pink robe. At the moment, she looks the furthest thing from a federal agent as you can get.

"I wasn't sure what you would like," I explain.

"You haven't eaten?" she asks.

"I was waiting for you."

"Oh," she mutters, going over to the pot of coffee I just made and pouring herself a cup into a giant mug that actually says, "*I like big mugs and I cannot lie.*" How ironic is that since I used lyrics from the same old song on my fake dating profile? Is that why she swiped right so fast, because we had that common interest? Not to mention the bag of Funyuns in the cabinet...

Peyton takes a sip of her coffee and stares at me over the top of the mug silently.

"Dig in," I tell her. Standing up, I motion with my hand for her to grab one of the plates I pulled out. After she comes over and finishes picking through the selection first, I pile the cold food on my plate and then pop it in the microwave for a few seconds to heat it up. Peyton sits down and eats hers cold.

"Do you normally restrain your one-night stands while you go get them breakfast?" she asks after we're almost done eating, and I'm relieved that we're past the tears and to the joking portion of my stupid shenanigans.

"No," I reply with a grin. Tossing my fork down on my empty plate, I admit to her, "I don't normally stay all night. And I *never* buy anyone breakfast."

"Wow. Don't I feel special," Peyton replies sarcastically.

"Last night you wore me out, so I had no choice but to sleep over when you collapsed on top of me. Treating you to breakfast seemed like the least I could do to say thank you for the best sex of my life."

True story—my dick is actually raw after the number of times she demanded we use it, but it was so worth it. Good thing she had an unopened box of condoms handy.

Wait. If I'm sore, then she has to be hurting in her lady parts.

"Today's the second day you've made me miss work." Peyton glowers at me rather than respond to my compliment. And I've had a lot of sex so that's really saying something.

"Did you call in sick?" I ask.

"Yes."

"Good, so we can go back to bed—" I start.

"No."

"To get some more *sleep* is what I was gonna say before you interrupted me," I grumble. "I bet I'm just as sore as you are."

"I seriously doubt it," she mutters.

"I didn't hear any complaints last night," I point out, and don't miss the smile she tries to hide behind her big coffee mug.

"My ride is on the way," I assure her.

"Good," she replies.

"Great. It'll take another hour for him to get here, though." I get to my feet and go wash my plate in the sink before standing it up on the drying rack. "If you need me, I'll be in your bed, *sleeping*," I tell Peyton before I head off down the hallway.

CHAPTER EIGHT

Peyton

Dalton is the most infuriating man I have ever met.

And yet, I nearly get up and follow him to my bedroom like a lost puppy.

Instead of giving in to his good looks or charm, still angry at him for leaving me restrained for what felt like days but I now know was only minutes, I decide to spend my sick day cleaning, even though I'm incredibly exhausted after not getting much sleep for the last two nights because of one hot bastard.

I have no clue what led to my emotional breakdown. I mean, yes, thinking you may die handcuffed to your own bed before someone finds you is worthy of freaking out about, but the tears? That's not my usual style. I'm tough as nails. I can handle any fucking thing life throws at me, including a cheating husband who wasted years of my life.

So why did I lose my shit because Dalton left me? It had to be because of the vulnerable position he had me in. He's a stranger and an outlaw biker, so I'm mostly angry at myself for falling into bed so quickly with him when I shouldn't have ever wanted him.

I'm lost in my thoughts, dusting off the television in the living room, when the doorbell rings, nearly startling the piss out of me.

Before I can calm my heart rate down enough to go answer it, Dalton comes strolling through the living room like he owns it. His blond hair is even more mussed than before and for some strange reason, it works for him.

"That's my ride," he says with a yawn. "It's been fun. Call me on Henry's number if you want a repeat of last night." After giving me a sexy wink, he wraps an arm around my back to pull me against his body and kiss my cheek again, way too sweet a gesture for the pornographic things we did to each other last night. Then he lets me go and walks out the door, without a care in the world.

And while I know I shouldn't ever tell anyone about what I did with him last night, there's no way I can keep the last twenty-four hours a secret from my best friend.

"*Y*ou *did what?*" Quincey shouts after she brings me lunch on her break and I tell her about the events of the previous day.

"I got my laptop back," I point out.

"After you kidnapped a man and held him hostage for it?" she asks, taking a seat in the same chair at the kitchen table that Dalton occupied just hours earlier.

"Well, yes, but what else was I supposed to do?" I ask, sitting down across from her.

"You handcuffed him and brought him here?"

"Yes," I answer.

"And held him at gunpoint?"

"Uh-huh," I answer, chewing nervously on my thumbnail since that sounds bad when it's said aloud.

"So, a member of a motorcycle gang not only knows where you live but could come back for revenge?" Quincey points out while setting down a container of Chinese food in front of me.

"Dalton wouldn't do that," I tell her.

"You're one hundred percent certain about that?"

"No, but I don't think he would."

"Peyton, you need to move, like now," she says. "You could come stay with me."

"I'm not scared of him," I assure her, even though I nearly have a panic attack every time I recall those minutes this morning where I thought I was going to die naked and restrained to my bed.

"You should be!" Quincey says. She even gets up and rushes over to peek out the blinds in the living room. "Those MC guys are all about vengeance. Haven't you ever watched *Sons of Anarchy*?"

"It's fine," I tell her with a roll of my eyes.

"How do you know that for sure, though?" she asks, retaking her seat.

"Because he stayed here with me last night, all night, voluntarily," I blurt out.

Jaw gaping, she looks at me for several silent movements before her lips curl into a grin. "You *slept* with him?"

"Yeah, I did," I admit with a grin.

"And? How was it, finally ending the long, four hundred days of famine?"

"I don't know," I answer. "Guess that depends on which time you're asking about."

"How many times?" she shrieks.

"Several."

"Several?"

"Five times," I answer. "That I remember."

"Holy shit!" she exclaims.

"I don't know how it happened. After I let him go, he sort of propositioned me, and I didn't say no. In fact, I actually begged for it."

"Wow," Quincey says. "So you *want* him to come back."

"Of course not," I huff. "That would be incredibly stupid."

"Yes, you do. You wouldn't turn him away if he did, would you?"

"I should," I reply. "Like you said, he's an outlaw in a motorcycle gang that I'm investigating for multiple murders and a deadly arson. He's dangerous and I could lose my job."

"Yeah, you could, genius. What were you thinking, Peyton?"

"You saw him. Would you have turned him down?" I ask.

"Absolutely not, but I'm just a paralegal who can work anywhere. You're an *agent*! Now your entire career could be in jeopardy."

"No, it's not, because it's over. I won't see him again," I assure her, even though I can't help but think I haven't seen the last of Dalton Brady just yet.

CHAPTER NINE

Dalton

I t's been two long weeks since the computer heist, and fuck, I really want to see Peyton again. Which goes completely against the rules I made for myself when I was seventeen: One, don't ever care about a woman more than she cares about you, and two, never get so attached that you can't walk away without ever looking back.

Not to mention that Peyton is the enemy of the MC, and she lives two hours away. A woman like her would never want to be with an outlaw biker like me for more than a night anyway.

Would she?

She sure as hell hasn't called me. And there's not much I can offer her that a common sex toy can't handle.

Alone in my apartment at the clubhouse, where I've spent way too much time lately whenever I'm not at the nursing home, I turn my bare back to the bathroom mirror. I try to avoid looking at the raised, circular scar of the old bullet wound, the one that almost paralyzed, and nearly killed, me. Instead, I'm more interested in the white scratches that run vertically through my Savage Kings tattoo. The ones that are almost healed. Oddly enough, I want a new set, a reminder of the best sex of my life.

Peyton was a hellcat after I kissed her, and she finally gave in to me.

If I showed up at her doorstep, would she invite me in or tell me to go to hell?

That's the question I've been asking myself over and over again. I've been too chicken shit to go see for myself because I'm pretty sure that even if she wanted me, she'd turn me down, thanks to the fact that we play on opposite sides of the law.

Too bad I'm not Henry, the attorney.

She wanted him so damn bad she let him eat her out in public on a first date. I'm guessing that's not something that straight-laced ATF agent Peyton Bradley normally does with a guy she just met on a dating app.

Shit, that reminds me...

I pull out my phone, log into the phony account I made, and *boom*, there she is. Not only is she still on the dating app, but she changed her profile picture, which means she's been on since the two of us were together. Guess she's looking for another handsome attorney to come sweep her off her feet, or bend her over her backseat.

Peyton's probably been chatting with tons of guys and meeting them in that same damn white-collar bar.

Will she go to her car to make out with those fuckers too? Or worse, will she take them home and dig her claws into their backs while they fuck her against the wall and every other way humanly possible in her bed?

Not if I have anything to say about it, she won't. I just have to remind myself the only reason I want to see her again is to fuck her. Nothing more.

I can't afford to let myself start caring about her.

Peyton

"Do you like oysters?" my latest fail from the dating app asks me while I quickly swallow down the rest of my vodka martini and beg the bartender for another.

Over the last two weeks, I've met three different men for drinks. None of which have made it to the second round, which would be meeting again to have dinner. The previous two, I walked out on after about ten minutes.

So why am I even bothering tonight?

Because I'm hoping to find someone, anyone, that will take my mind off a big, sexy, blond biker. Dalton's been a constant, nagging thought ever since the morning he strolled out of my house, leaving me with a night full of memories that never seem to stop popping up at random moments throughout the day, even when I'm at work.

Sighing, since forgetting Dalton is starting to seem like an impossible feat, I start to answer the boring man's question with a "hell no" on the oysters when someone suddenly lifts the back of my hair to the side...and places a damp kiss on my neck that makes me shiver all the way down to my toes.

"What the—" I start to say while craning my neck around to see who would...*oh shit.*

"There's my beautiful *wife*," Dalton says with a grin before he lets my hair go to grab my left hand from the bar. He *tsks*. "Did you lose your wedding ring again, kitten?"

"Ah, it was, um, nice to meet you," my date from hell says before he scrambles off his stool and runs out the door. Dalton's height and size must have been intimidating to the balding midget.

"What are you doing here?" I hiss at the biker, trying not to get distracted by his beautiful face.

"Saving you from having to waste another second talking to the dwarf," he says with a chuckle as he pops the front button on his navy-blue suit jacket and takes the man's seat, like a king lowering himself onto his throne.

"Is that the only suit you own?" I ask, trying to look and sound disinterested in his presence, even though the second I saw him, a jolt of longing seared through me from my head down to my toes.

After over a year of celibacy, you wouldn't think two weeks would seem like a long time to not have sex. Yet, after the amazing night with Dalton, I've been desperate for more. You better believe my vibrator has been working overtime, but it's just not the same, since it never talks to me or touches me the same way...

"Why, yes, it is," Dalton answers as he preens and straightens his suit jacket. "No reason to buy more when this one worked just fine on you. Although, there are some scuffs on the knees that the dry cleaner couldn't get out after I—"

"Why are you here?" I ask, interrupting him when he starts to bring up what we did the night in the parking garage. "And save the bullshit about rescuing me from a shitty date."

"So, it *was* shitty? I knew it," he replies with a smirk.

"Answer the question."

"Fine," he huffs before he places a hand on the back of my stool to lean in closer to me, engulfing me in his masculine cologne and clean scent that still holds a hint of leather from his recently worn cut. "It's been two long weeks, and I couldn't go one more day without seeing your beautiful...pussy."

Smiling despite myself, I place my palm on his cheek and push his too handsome face away from me.

"So, you drove two hours for sex?" I ask.

"No, I drove two hours for an entire night of enthusiastic love-making with a smoking hot ATF agent."

"Awful presumptuous, aren't you?" I mutter, even though his charming ass is already wearing me down, no matter how apathetic I try to sound.

"That wasn't a no, so yeah, I'm feeling pretty good about the odds of getting you naked and fucking you like an animal again."

"You shouldn't be here," I tell him honestly, glancing away before he can see my blush.

"Still not a no," he points out. "Besides, here in this white-collar bar, I'm just Henry Aycock, good old trustworthy personal injury attorney."

"Right," I drawl sarcastically with a roll of my eyes.

"You can't deny that you were into Henry." Dalton leans in close to me again and rubs the tip of his nose along the column of my neck, causing goose bumps to race down my arms. Whispering close to my ear, he says, "All Henry had to do was kiss you and you were ready to bend over for him."

"*Henry* is nothing but a lying thief," I reply, my hands shoving against his hard chest to put some distance between us. Dalton is so freaking dangerous because he's damn near impossible to resist, especially in such close proximity.

Placing his free hand on my knee and sliding it up the thigh of my suit pants, he says, "*Henry* apologizes for the briefcase mix-up. In fact, he would love to get on his knees again and make it up to you by kissing every inch of flesh that lies underneath your panties. I'm betting they're already getting a little wet..."

Taking a sip of my martini to collect my thoughts after that naughty offer, I decide to turn the tables to try and catch the cocky bastard off guard. Meeting Dalton's intense blue gaze and holding it, I say, "I think I would rather get on my knees and torture *Henry* first."

"Torture would be saying shit like that to a desperate man and not backing it up," Dalton instantly counters.

So, he's desperate for me too? How is that possible?

"*Henry* doesn't have any objections to following through with that kind of torture, though?" I ask.

"Fuck no, kitten. It's his favorite brand of torture," he replies. "In fact, if you really wanted to torture him, you would give him a little tease right here, right now, in the bathroom. Then make him wait until he got back to your place to let him come inside of you."

"Who said I wouldn't let him come in my mouth?" I ask with a smirk.

Swearing under his breath, Dalton grabs my forearm as he jumps from his seat, pulling me behind him toward the bar's bathrooms. Thankfully, tonight, I left my laptop at the office, so I don't have to worry about hauling it around or having someone steal it.

We're in the women's bathroom a second later. Dalton turns the lock to keep anyone from interrupting and then he's pushing on my shoulders, guiding me down to my knees in front of him. After I'm in position, his trembling hands work to get his belt and pants undone. Seeing him look so frantic for relief that I'll give him sends me on one hell of a power trip. Now it's my turn to make *him* beg.

A ragged gust of air puffs out of his mouth when he finally frees his cock. He stands there, towering over me and stroking his swelling shaft while looking down at me through heavy-lidded eyes. God, he's so sexy that I want to scarf him down my throat. But first, he deserves a little payback.

"I think I've changed my mind," I tell him with my head tilted back to see his face better.

"No. No, no, no." He groans while he continues to work his hand up and down his cock. "Can't you just give it a little lick?" he asks before rubbing the fat head over my lips.

I lean back to answer, moving away from his big cock's reach. "I'm still a little angry at you. Might bite it off."

"Come on, Peyton," he whines as he keeps jerking himself off. "All I've had is my own hand for two fucking weeks. You've ruined me for other women."

"*I've* ruined you?" I repeat, my words heavy with disbelief.

"Do you know how many club sluts I've turned down in the last two weeks?"

"How many?" I ask curiously, trying not to focus too hard-on his use of the word *sluts* to describe them.

"Nine," he answers. "It's been slow at the clubhouse since everyone's shacking up lately."

Jesus. Nine women have tried to sleep with him in two weeks? And he calls that *slow*? That's insane but believable.

"Why did you turn them down?" I question, even though I don't entirely buy his celibate claim.

"So that when I saw you again, if you asked me, I could tell you I haven't been with anyone else," he says.

"That's a good answer," I tell him, almost believing it. "So good, that I may finally give you that little lick you're so desperate for."

Leaning forward, I circle the tip of my tongue around the head of his cock like it's an ice cream cone before I lap up the drops of moisture leaking from his slit. The more I lick, the more salty goodness I taste.

"Does it hurt?" I ask before I run my tongue up his length and over his fingers that are still stroking.

"God, yes," he grunts.

"Then we better get you home fast," I tell him. I open my mouth to take in just the tip, stopping at the raised circumcision rim, and suck hard enough to make Dalton shout a curse to the ceiling before I pull away.

Getting to my feet, I remove his hands from his hard dick to shove it back into his pants and zip him up before I unlock the door and walk out, knowing he'll be right behind me.

CHAPTER TEN

Dalton

Peyton wasn't joking about torturing me.

I'm lying on her bed with my suit jacket off, dress shirt unbuttoned, pants open, and wrists restrained by her handcuffs to the slat in her headboard. Her amazing mouth keeps bringing me to the edge of orgasm before she pulls away from my dick, only to restart the tormenting all over again.

Did I mention she's only wearing a lacy pink bra and matching thong panties?

"Please, please, please," I beg, my bare heels digging into the mattress when she kisses her way up my abs and back down again. The first thing Peyton did after I was restrained was to take off my shoes and socks and tickle the soles of my feet. The woman is pure evil.

"Please what?" Peyton asks.

"Please suck me off until I come!" I exclaim in a rush as I jerk against the handcuffs so hard it's a wonder I haven't ripped out the wooden slat yet. If my hands were free, I would've jacked myself off an hour ago, which is exactly why she took them away from me.

"Haven't you ever heard of delayed gratification?" Peyton looks up and asks smugly before placing a kiss on my pelvis, just above the manscaping line. The ends of her long blonde hair continue to tickle my thighs and dick in a way that's making me crazy.

"You've delayed long enough!" I shout in frustration. If she delays much longer, my balls may rupture. I could very well have erectile dysfunction after this type of abuse.

"Almost," she agrees. "I'm making you suffer twice as long as you left me restrained."

So, this is my punishment.

I should've known, when we were in the bar and she offered to get on her knees, it was too good to be true.

"Actually," Peyton starts, before she sits back on her heels and fake yawns, "I'm getting tired and I *do* have to be at work early tomorrow. Think I'll call it a night."

"I'm sorry, okay!" I yell. "I came back!" I remind her, not just that morning, but tonight, because I wanted to see her. Hell, I *needed* to see her again. I hate myself for admitting as much to her, but the words start pouring out of my mouth, desperate for her to give me some relief. "You're all I've thought about for fourteen fucking days, woman!"

Scoffing, Peyton says, "You and I both know you only came for one thing."

Squeezing my eyes shut to try and focus on breathing through the agony in my lower body, I lay out all of the reasons why I came to see her tonight, even though I told myself it was just to fuck. "I didn't come for one thing. I want to sleep with you and have you rake your fingernails down my back again so hard it bleeds. Then, I want to shower with you in the morning, so that I can wash your hair. After that, I want to feed you breakfast and make plans to see you again over coffee in your ridiculously large mug. While you're at work tomorrow, I want you to think about me and miss me—"

My words end on a choking gasp when her warm, wet mouth closes around my cock. Peyton sucks me so hard and fast that the building pleasure of over an hour of torture finally bursts free from the dam. My spine bows off the mattress as I gasp for air like a drowning man through the pulses of ecstasy so strong my toes may be permanently curled.

"Feel better?" Peyton asks. And when I'm able to blink my eyes open again, she's straddling me, her hands gripping my shoulders with her face right in front of mine.

"Oh yeah," I tell her with a lazy, satisfied smile.

"Good," she replies before pressing her lips to mine. After several soft kisses, she pulls away to unlock my wrists from the cuffs.

"That was so worth the wait," I tell her when I can finally wrap my arms around her back and hold her. "Now it's your turn."

"That's okay," she says. "I got myself off twice, once while I was teasing you and then again when you finished."

"Wow," I mutter in surprise, hating I missed that while I was too busy balancing on a tightrope of pain and pleasure.

"Let's get some rest. We can get up early enough for you to... wash my hair and fuck me in the shower before I have to go to work."

"Best idea ever, kitten," I agree.

Several minutes later, Peyton still hasn't made a move to get off of me. Which is fine, I could probably sleep with her straddling me. Peyton blankets are nice...

But then her brow furrows and she lowers her eyes to where her hands are gripping the sides of my open shirt collar, like she's suddenly a million miles away.

"What is it?" I ask, trying to read her sudden change in expression.

"Why couldn't you really be Henry the attorney?" she asks sadly, making my guts twist into a knot from the amount of sadness in her voice because I'm not the man she wants. "This would be so much easier..."

"Seems like this *is* pretty damn easy," I point out. Before she decides to throw me out of her bed because of a crisis of conscious, I tell her, "Come on, kitten. You have to admit that the whole forbidden affair thing is what makes being with me so hot and exciting. If I were just Henry, the boring but handsome attorney, you would've fallen asleep by now."

Cracking a small smile, she says, "Not if Henry was into kinky shit like handcuffs."

"Oh, Henry is a complete control freak. He'd never let a woman put him in such a compromising position, even for an award-winning blowjob."

"Maybe," she says. "But I wouldn't be worried about losing my job with Henry."

"How am I gonna make you lose your job?" I ask in confusion.

"You want me to drop the investigation of the Savage Kings," Peyton reminds me.

"Yeah? So?"

"If I do that, then I'm not doing the job I was hired to do. Especially if your club hurts someone else."

"Listen, babe," I tell her, reaching up to cup the side of her face. "I can promise you that the Kings don't hurt anyone unless they deserve it."

"It's not your job to decide who deserves it and who doesn't!" she exclaims, pulling away from me to sit up straighter, while still straddling my hips in nothing but her bra and panties.

Propping myself up on my elbows, I say, "So, if someone killed your husband and kid, you would sit on your hands and wait for what? A trial, years later, if the cops were even able to arrest the bastard responsible in the first place?"

"Yes! What if you went after the wrong person?"

"We're not a bunch of hotheaded idiots," I assure her. "We wouldn't go after someone if we weren't one hundred percent certain they were guilty."

"So, you think you're all infallible?" she asks.

"I think we do our due diligence."

"This is what I'm talking about," she mutters as she reaches up to push her hair out of her face. "We'll never agree on this."

"So, we agree to disagree," I tell her.

"And then there's the fact that I don't do casual relationships. I'm not a casual person like you," she adds, doing a complete one-eighty on the topic, like she's checking off little boxes for all the reasons why she should throw me out of her bed tonight.

"How do you know I'm a casual person?" I ask, even though *casual* may as well be my middle name.

The silent but deadly look she gives me says she's not buying it.

"Fine, so I am. I *was*. But if casual is all I wanted right now, don't you think it would've been a lot easier for me to get my dick sucked from one of the club sluts who party right above my apartment rather than drive two hours to see a woman who may or may not slap me or shoot me on sight?"

"Why did you come back?" she asks. "I can't help feeling like this is just some kind of game to you."

"It's not," I tell her sincerely. Jesus, is she gonna make me hand over my balls? May as well. I don't ever let myself get this attached to a woman, much less tell her shit. For whatever reason, though, I admit to Peyton, "Honestly, I have no fucking clue why I can't forget you. But I can't. And I don't want you to forget me either."

Her face softens as she looks me in the eye. "It's pretty hard to forget the first man I was with after my husband."

"Husband?" I repeat as I jackknife into a sitting position, my heart trying to jump out of my chest. How could I make the same mistake twice in this fucking lifetime? "You're married?"

"No," she says with a shake of her head. "Divorced."

"You're divorced," I mutter, and my shoulders slump in relief when I belatedly remember her mentioning that she has an ex-husband the first night in the bar. Thank fuck. "How long were you married?"

"Six years," she answers. "We met the last year of graduate school and got married right before we joined the agency."

"What happened?"

"He's an agent too," she explains. "And he worked undercover. Often."

"So, distance was the problem?"

"No, him fucking women while he was undercover to 'play up the part' was the problem."

"Oh," I mutter. "He cheated on you?"

"Frequently," she responds with a nod of her head.

"How did you find out what was going on?" I ask.

"His partner told me he thought he was screwing around. So, then I went through his things when he was in the shower and found his *second* phone that had texts and voicemails from other women. Ones that left no doubt..."

"Wow."

"Yeah," Peyton says. "So that's why I was glad to leave Georgia for a while when they offered me this temporary position."

"How long have you been separated?" I inquire.

"Over a year ago."

"A year?" I echo. "So I'm the first person you've slept with...*in a year?*"

"Over a year," she replies again. "And don't look so smug."

"I can't help it. I have a naturally smug face," I tease, while inside, I'm doing cartwheels because she picked me for some crazy reason after waiting a year to get over her ex-husband.

"What Jack did was a huge betrayal. And if he could cheat on me after being married for six years, then it was hard to think about being with a stranger and expecting him to not do the same thing to me right away."

"Is that your way of telling me that you don't want me to fuck anyone else?" I ask.

"Like you would do anything I asked," she mutters with a roll of her eyes.

"I would, if you tell me that sex with me is better than it was with your cheating husband."

She's silent for so long, I nearly give up. Finally, she says, "Sex with you is so much better than with my cheating bastard husband. Which makes sense."

"Why is that?" I ask.

"Because you've probably been with ten times as many women as him."

"Practice makes perfect," I reply.

"Yeah, I guess it does," Peyton agrees.

"And you have my word that I won't fool around with anyone else as long as we're seeing each other," I tell her, promising her something I've never offered a woman before.

It's stupid because agreeing to be monogamous is like one step away from having feelings, something I can't afford to catch. Still, I don't want to stop fucking Peyton just yet. Who would walk away from the best sex of their life when they finally find it?

"Right," she agrees at my assurances, sounding sarcastic and doubtful that I'll keep my word before she climbs off of me. "We better get some sleep." After she turns off the light, she pulls the covers over us and then cuddles up to my chest. "Goodnight."

"Goodnight," I say, and then I try to drift off to sleep, wondering if she'll let me stay over tomorrow night too.

It's a slippery slope I'm on, but even if my life depended on it, I don't think I could stop myself from seeing Peyton.

CHAPTER ELEVEN

Peyton

For the last few weeks, I've been living my usual boring life during the day. At work, I bust my ass interviewing confidential informants, testifying in court as needed for cases I helped blow open after I first moved here, and investigating potential criminals.

Then at night, it's like I become someone else with Dalton. Someone I don't even recognize, but who I sort of love. He sets me free from all of the insecurities I've had for so long because it's impossible to feel anything but sexy when I'm with him and he's talking dirty to me while stripping me out of my clothes within seconds of seeing me.

Afterward, we lie in bed, talking and joking while recovering for the next round, since one time never seems to be enough for either of us.

I've never had a situation like this with a man that revolves solely around sex. If I didn't know any better, I would almost say we're in a relationship since Dalton stays over at least four or five of the seven nights each week.

The only problem is that in the morning, when the sun comes up and we climb out of bed, there's always an enormous elephant in the room. Dalton slips on his ever-present leather cut, and I know he's going to drive back to the coast to do...whatever it is he does in the MC while I put on my suit and head into the federal building to do my job that centers around arresting criminals.

"Bradley," Stan Sommers, the Assistant United States Attorney that's over the criminal division says in his deep authoritative voice, startling me when he walks into my small office since I'm only here temporarily.

"Yes, sir. What can I do for you?" I ask, trying not to panic and think the worst, that he somehow found out about my stolen laptop or the fact that an outlaw MC hacked into our system.

"Just wanted to drop by and see how the investigations are coming along," he says, leaning a meaty shoulder covered in a white dress shirt against the door frame and sipping on his steaming cup of coffee. His posture all but screams cool and laidback, so I'm going to take that as a sign that I'm not fucked.

"Things are going well," I tell him. "I've been working with some of the local law enforcement agencies on the motorcycle gangs you had on the list, comparing notes with them to cover all of our bases."

"Great," he says. "What about the Savage Kings?"

"Ah, what about them?" I ask, hoping the fact that I'm close to a full-blown panic attack isn't visible on my face or in the rapid movements of my chest.

"Anything concrete that we can tie them to?" he questions.

"Um, no, sir. Not yet at least."

"Keep digging. We can't afford to let them get away with the charges they've been building up all around them. It's possible that local agencies are helping them cover their tracks."

"Right, of course," I tell him. "Maybe I should, um, take off for the coast for a few days to meet with the local departments. Sitting down face-to-face with them, I may be able to get a better feel for where their allegiances lie."

"Great idea. Send me your notes while you're gone," he says.

"Will do, sir," I agree before he finally turns around and walks away.

Blowing out a breath of relief, I pull out my cell phone and consider sending Dalton a message to let him know I'll be in his neck of the woods in a few hours. Instead, I decide to surprise him and just see what he's up to during the days after he leaves my bed.

~

Dalton

"W here have you been disappearing to every night?" Reece asks when he wanders into my apartment in the basement of the clubhouse.

"Out," I say, without looking away from the accounting program on my computer screen. The end of the month is approaching quickly, and I'm behind because I've been spending my nights with Peyton and my days visiting my old man. I try not to think too hard about how being with Peyton makes getting through the tough days a little easier...

"Out where?"

"None of your fucking business," I mutter.

"Sort of is my business, and the MC's, when you're spending more time with the ATF agent than you are here."

Finally, turning my gaze to him, I narrow my eyes and tell him, "I handle my shit for the MC. And I don't need anyone's permission or approval for where I want to spend my nights."

"She's using you," he tells me, driving an imaginary knife right through my guts. "Just as soon as you slip up and give her the intel she needs, she'll take us all down."

"Peyton doesn't give a shit about the MC," I snap at him. "She agreed to drop the investigation against us, thanks to me."

"Oh really?" Reece asks with a chuckle, his arms crossing over his chest and a know-it-all smugness plastered across his face.

"Yeah, really. The Savage Kings don't have anything to worry about with the feds."

"You're absolutely sure about that?" he questions.

"Yes!" I exclaim.

"How sure? Would you say a hundred percent?" he inquires.

Jesus, why can't he leave this shit alone?

"Yeah, I am one hundred fucking percent certain that the feds are through with the MC!"

"Well, in that case, I hate to break it to you, brother, but you're completely fucking wrong."

"Wrong?" I huff. "How the hell am I wrong?"

"Because your agent has been parked right outside the clubhouse for over two hours."

"She is?" I ask, pushing back my rolling computer chair to get to my feet. "She could just be here to see me."

"Right, like a friendly, personal visit?" he offers.

"Exactly," I tell him, even though I'm not entirely sure why Peyton would show up here and not call to let me know...

"Then why did Jade just call Torin and tell him she has a meeting with her tomorrow?" Reece asks.

"Shit," I mutter as I scrub my palm over my face. Jade is Chase and Torin's stepsister, and the local sheriff.

"You need to find out what's going on, and then get the hell away from her before you fuck up and take us all down with you," he warns.

"That's not gonna happen." I grab my cut from the foot of the bed and slip my arms through it. "Just give me a few days to talk to her," I say, then smirk to hide my real concern. "And could you not

96

tell Torin or anyone that she's lurking outside? Maybe she's just stalking me."

"Yeah, a few days," he agrees. "But if any more feds start circling outside like vultures, I'll have to take it to the table."

"Fine," I agree with a sigh.

CHAPTER TWELVE

Peyton

Four hours or so after I left the office, I'm still sitting outside the *Savage Asylum* with a pair of binoculars, watching and waiting. Various guys in leather cuts come and go on Harleys, some with beards like the club's logo, some clean-shaven like Dalton. During the slow periods, I make a few phone calls to the Carteret Sheriff's office and the Wilmington PD to set up appointments to meet with leadership over the next few days.

All afternoon while I wait, I don't see Dalton, but his unique bike, blue among all the black, sits in the lot, so I'm guessing he's inside.

My phone rings right on time, a few minutes after five o'clock, which is when he knows I'm usually leaving the office. How is it that I've already come to start anticipating his call after seeing him for just a few weeks?

"Hello," I answer, even though I'm pretty certain it's Dalton calling from the "unavailable" phone number.

"Whatcha doin'?" he asks casually, but just the simple phrase makes me smile.

"Just leaving work," I reply like usual.

"Good. Want me to head over?" he offers. He's been spending almost every night with me. Is it stupid of me to think that if he's in my bed, he can't be with anyone else? It is because he has the whole day to screw around with women here in Emerald Isle before coming back to my place. But I have yet to smell another woman's perfume on him. He could just be showering after his day romps. *Like he showers each morning before leaving you*, my heart throws in my face.

"You don't have to come over tonight," I tell him.

"Well, what if I really, really want to?" he lowers his voice and asks coolly, making my hormones cheer.

"I want to see you too, but I'm not gonna be home," I reply.

"You're not?" he asks, sounding surprised. "So where will you be?"

"Girls' night out with my friend."

"You're going to the bar to pick up guys with Quincey?" he asks, his words crisper, almost like he's jealous.

"We're just going out to dinner. No guys," I further my lie.

"So, then I could come over afterward…" he offers.

"Not tonight. It'll probably be late."

"You know I don't have a curfew, kitten," he says with a chuckle.

"I know, but some people have to get up early and go to work tomorrow morning. The later you get started, the later I'll be awake."

"I could just come over and sleep in the same bed as you, no funny business," he says, which we both know is a lie. There's always funny business when the two of us are together. Usually several rounds before we're finally able to stop mauling each other and fall asleep.

"Maybe this weekend," I tell him.

"This weekend?" Dalton exclaims. "What about tomorrow night? And Thursday night? You have plans then too?"

"I'll be traveling. For work," I admit.

"Alone?" he asks.

"Yes."

"I don't think that's a good idea," he grumbles.

"I can take care of myself," I assure him. "I'm a federal agent with extensive training, remember? There's nothing I can't handle."

"Oh really?" he asks. "No one can sneak up behind you and take you by surprise?"

"No," I answer, but still look up in my rearview mirror just to check.

"You sure about that?" he asks, and then there's a knock on my driver side window that makes me gasp so suddenly that I nearly choke on the intake of air. Dark clothes are all I can see at first until I glance up and see his smug face.

"Even if I hadn't heard your gasp of surprise, I would've seen you jump," the jerk says into the phone with a grin stretched across his face.

I end the phone call and push the button to roll down my window.

"Were you trying to give me a heart attack?" I ask him.

"No, I was proving a point and trying to see if you would be straight with me. You shouldn't be out here alone," he says, leaning his crossed forearms on the windowsill to duck his head inside to steal a kiss from my cheek.

"Why? Because the Savage Kings are dangerous?" I question, threading my fingers through the top of his soft, messy blond hair just because I can. Going all day at work without touching him or seeing him is harder than it should be.

"Possibly, if they feel threatened by some feds," he answers. Stealing another kiss, this time from my lips, he says, "We've been watching you watch us from the surveillance cameras."

"Oh," I mutter since I thought I was parked far enough away from the property. "And, let me guess, there's a back door?"

"Yep," Dalton answers before his lips press against mine again.

"So, now will you tell me the truth about what the hell you're doing out here?"

"I'm in town for a few days," I explain.

"Investigating us?" he pulls back and looks at me through narrowed blue eyes. "I thought you agreed to lay off of us in exchange for your laptop."

"Yes, *I* did. The man I work for, the U.S. Attorney, didn't though. He wants me to keep digging, so that's what I'm doing."

"Do you think that if you sit here long enough, you'll catch us breaking the law?" he asks sarcastically.

"No, I just stopped by while I set up a few meetings in the area," I respond honestly.

"Meetings with whom?" he asks, but I just blink silently at him in response. "Fine, don't tell me," he huffs before cutting his eyes over to the bar. "Where are you staying while you're in town?"

"I have a hotel room at the, um, *Jolly Roger*. There aren't many hotels around here, and most are booked this time of year."

A bigger grin spreads over Dalton's face before he says, "You, an ATF agent, are staying at the *Jolly Roger*?"

"Yeah? Why?" I ask.

"Oh, nothing," he says, still smirking. "It's just that the Kings own the hotel."

"They do? How did I not know that?"

"We bought it through dummy corps," Dalton responds, then points his index finger at me. "But you can't use any of that against us. It's all completely legit. We had attorneys set it up."

"I'm sure you did," I scoff. "So that's how you launder your money?"

"I think I've given you enough of our secrets," he says before his gaze lowers to the front of my blouse where the proof of how much my body enjoys his close proximity is obvious, even through my bra. "Are you headed to the hotel now?"

"Maybe," I answer.

"Why don't I follow you? You know, to watch your back to make sure no one fucks with you while you're in town."

"You think someone could fuck with me?" I ask.

Blowing out a breath, he says, "Our pres has a new family after losing his first one violently. I wouldn't put much past Torin when it comes to protecting the shit he loves."

"And he loves the MC?"

"Damn right, he does," he agrees seriously before instantly turning playful again when he reaches inside the vehicle to strum his thumb over my left nipple. "Besides, I want to be the only one who...fucks with you."

Sometimes I wish he wasn't so good at fucking with me. The things his body can do in bed should be illegal. I grow a little more addicted to him each and every time.

"Fine, follow me?" I ask, like it wasn't already a given he would be spending the night in my room.

"I'll meet you there," he says with a wink before he slaps his palm on my windowsill and strolls off toward the row of bikes in the bar parking lot.

Dalton

I'm trusting Reece not to tell Torin or any of the other guys about Peyton watching the clubhouse. The two of us made an agreement. He won't spill because I assured him she wasn't going to cause us any problems.

Then, I find out she's here meeting with Jade, and who the hell knows who else, because her boss doesn't want to give up on screwing us over. Now I don't know *what* to think.

Was I wrong to believe that giving her the laptop back, along with a few good fucks, would be enough to convince her to stop investigating the Savage Kings? Maybe I gave myself too much credit. It's possible I've been too busy falling for her that I didn't stop to think that maybe she doesn't feel the same way about me.

Could this just be sex between us while she uses me to bring down the MC? I've already told her too much about the club, I know, but nothing that would come back and screw us over. I don't think...

Those are the thoughts that are haunting me a few minutes later, after I get Peyton checked into the hotel and up to her room. We both get naked in a blur of flying clothes before she kisses me and rides me down on the bed.

"Um, Dalton?" Peyton asks when she pulls back to look down at me.

"Yeah?" I answer.

"Are you okay?"

"I'm fucking a beautiful woman, why wouldn't I be?" I reply.

"You haven't touched me," she informs me, and I realize my arms are stretched out by my sides.

"Oh."

"And you're, ah, you're not..." Peyton lowers her eyes down my body.

"Not what?" I ask.

"You're not...aroused." She sits back on my thighs to reveal my limp dick.

"What the fuck?" I exclaim as I sit up and take my flaccid cock in my fist to give it a few strokes. Nothing happens. I'm naked and in bed, with a gorgeous woman straddling me, and I can't get hard. "This...this has never happened to me before. Ever."

"It's not a big deal," Peyton says, even though it clearly is a big fucking deal. I'm a man. This is what we do, dammit! God gave us long hard cocks to fuck women with! It's like our sole purpose on Earth!

"Do you want me to try using my mouth?" she offers while I sit there panicking.

"No," I answer without hesitation. Not being able to get it up for sex is bad enough. What if a blowjob can't even revive it? Having a limp dick in a woman's mouth is blasphemy. My ego would never recover from such a fall from grace.

"Wait, it was working this morning, right?" I ask Peyton.

"Ah, yeah. From behind in bed and then against the shower wall while you were washing my hair."

"Right," I agree, as I remember the sexy details of peeling her panties down to take her as soon as we woke up and being ready to go again before the water turned warm in the shower. Even those incredible memories don't have any effect on my sleeping cock.

"Don't worry about it, Dalton. It happens to all men," Peyton says when she climbs off of me, without getting what she came for, and lies down next to me on the mattress.

"No, it doesn't happen to me," I tell her. "Let me, ah, let me take care of you," I suggest, to take the attention off of my failure to perform and because I want to make Peyton feel good, even if we can't feel good at the same time.

"You don't have to—" she starts to say, but I'm already diving between her legs, wedging my shoulders underneath her thighs. "Oh yeah," Peyton moans after I swipe my tongue over her clit. She spears her fingers through my hair and gives it a tug whenever I stop licking her in the way I know makes her crazy. That's the only reason I deviate my method, to tease her a little, get her to direct me as if she's in control.

By the third time her legs shake and clamp down on my ears, my dick is hard as a rock.

Thank fuck.

While Peyton's body and voice recovers from her most recent orgasm, I get off the bed and go retrieve a condom from my wallet. I tear open the foil with my teeth and sheath the rubber over my cock in record-breaking time.

When I'm back between Peyton's legs, lining up to take the plunge, she blinks her eyes open to look at me.

"Mmm," she murmurs and stretches her arms over her head. "You're so good at going down on me. Either you practiced a lot, or someone must have trained you well."

Aaand there goes my hard-on with the reminder of the woman who "trained" me.

"I'll be right back," I say before I climb off the bed and head for the bathroom, hoping Peyton didn't notice the condom or my deflating dick.

CHAPTER THIRTEEN

Peyton

I'm sitting in the Carteret County sheriff's office, bright and early Wednesday morning, half an hour early for our meeting. It's not like I had anything better to do.

Unlike most mornings, Dalton didn't stick around for a quickie in bed or in the shower. He was dressed and kissing me goodbye from beside the bed before I was able to fully blink my eyes open.

Now I have no clue if he was embarrassed about not being able to perform last night, or if he just didn't want me. Either way, I can't stop obsessing about what's going on with him and why he bailed so early.

Was that Dalton's way of blowing me off and ending this, whatever this is, between us? While I'm guessing that it's just sex for him, I've already gotten in too deep, thinking about him constantly and wanting to be near him, just to see what crazy comment he'll make next.

A smile spreads across my face whenever he comes to mind and, like a teenage girl, I can't stop myself from checking my phone a hundred times a day, even when I'm at work, to see if he's texted me or called. I check again while I sit in the waiting room but there's nothing new from him. So, like the obsessed, silly girl that I feel like around him, I scroll through and reread old messages, thinking of all the possible ways to interrupt them.

Shit. Is Dalton pissed because I'm in town having meetings about the Savage Kings?

"Agent Bradley?" the young, auburn-haired sheriff says when she opens her office door and steps out in her brown uniform. I toss my phone into my purse and get to my feet to go over and shake her hand. She offers me a friendly but professional smile. "It's nice to meet you."

"You too, Sheriff Horton," I reply.

"Come on in," she says before she leads the way to her office, shutting the door behind me after I'm inside. "Have a seat." She gestures toward one of the two visitor chairs before lowering herself into the high-back executive chair behind the desk.

"Thanks for agreeing to meet with me on such short notice," I tell her.

"No problem. Things are always pretty quiet around here, so there's plenty of time to meet with federal agents. What exactly is it that you wanted to discuss?"

"Oh, well, the U.S. Attorney for the Eastern District is investigating the Savage Kings MC, after several firearm and arson-related crimes."

"Oh," she mutters, her face falling and friendly demeanor changing quicker than I can snap my fingers.

"Is that a problem?" I ask.

"No," the sheriff answers with a shake of her head. "But I guess I should save you some time. My mother is married to Torin and Chase Fury's father."

"Wow," I say when I'm eventually able to pick up my gaping jaw. "So you're..."

"Their stepsister, yes," she answers with a nod. "Is there anything else I can help you with?"

"Can you give me any information about the Hector Cruz murder that resulted in the death of him and three of his men? Or the fire at a rival MC's bar? How about the shootout at the *Savage Asylum* and death of your stepbrother's wife?"

Looking only slightly annoyed at my rapid-fire questions, she begins to answer. "Our office determined that Hector Cruz was killed by his own men during a violent coup. As for the arson, well, you would have to talk to the Wilmington PD about that since it's out of my district, but I'm pretty sure they ruled the cause of the fire as a gas line exploding a meth lab." Pausing to take a deep breath, she goes on to say, "And the death of Kennedy Fury and my stepbrother's unborn son was incredibly tragic. While we were not able to link any suspects to the crime directly, the firearms and gun shells found at the scene of the Cruz shooting matched the one that killed Kennedy, so we have officially closed the case."

"And you don't think that the Savage Kings were involved in the murder of Hector Cruz and his men?" I ask, heavy with disbelief.

"There's no evidence that they were even in the vicinity. In fact, most of them were still in Las Vegas for my stepbrother's wedding."

"Isn't that convenient."

Eyes narrowing, the sheriff says, "It's the truth. Nothing convenient about it. There are airline records to back it up, and I'm sure you could obtain the video surveillance of the airports as well."

"Isn't it true that most of the members of the Savage Kings have criminal records?" I ask.

"About half, maybe," she answers with a shrug, like it's no big deal those same felons have formed a gang.

"Yet they aren't suspects for any of the violence that's happened up and down the coast lately?"

"No, they're not," Sheriff Horton answers with a stiff smile.

"What about Dalton Brady?" I ask, unable to help myself.

Reeling back in her seat, as if caught off guard by the random question, she says, "What about him?"

"Our intel leads us to believe that he's an officer in the MC. The treasurer or money launderer, perhaps?"

"I wouldn't know who is an officer, or what their responsibilities would be," she replies. "My stepbrothers and I don't discuss MC business at family dinners."

"Is there anything more that you *do* know about Dalton?" I inquire.

Sighing heavily, she leans back in her chair and crosses her arms over her chest. "All I know is that his father was one of the founding members. Why are you asking about him?"

"His father?" I repeat, ignoring her question, and she nods. "Is he still a member?" I ask since Dalton's never mentioned him, and the CI didn't have any notes about the senior Brady.

"No. If you can't ride, you can't vote," she answers easily, like it's a common phrase, making it sound like she knows more about the club's business than she's letting on.

"And Dalton's father can't ride?"

"Apparently not," the sheriff responds.

"Why is that?" I ask.

Sheriff Horton lifts one of her auburn eyebrows before she gets to her feet and says, "Is there anything else I can help you with today? Okay, thanks for stopping by," without giving me a chance to actually ask anything else.

I'm being dismissed.

Standing up, I tell her, "I appreciate your time." *Even though it was incredibly short.*

I barely step out of her office before she's behind me and shutting the door.

Protective much? Jeez.

My thoughts about the backward ways of this town come to a stop as soon as I walk down the steps of the sheriff's office and spot a sexy man in dark sunglasses, leaning his back against my SUV. His arms are crossed over his leather cut, along with his ankles. He looks like he's waiting for a photographer to come along, snap his photo, and slap it on the cover of a trendy magazine.

"How did you know I was here?" I ask curiously, since I didn't tell him who I was meeting with today or tomorrow.

"Jade called and gave Torin a heads-up yesterday after you set the meeting," he answers with a grin.

"Jade," I repeat, using her first name like he did so familiarly. "Well, wasn't that nice of her," I mutter sarcastically.

"They're family. What did you expect?" he asks when I'm standing right in front of him.

"I don't know. Maybe for her to be an officer of the law despite having family ties to a motorcycle club."

"Despite what you may think, she doesn't cut the MC any slack," Dalton responds.

"Bullshit."

"Okay, so she doesn't cut the MC *much* slack," he amends with a smirk.

"Whatever you say," I tell him, even though I'm starting to see why the sheriff would protect the guys in the MC if the rest are half as charming as Dalton. Which makes me ask, "Is the sheriff...close with any other members?"

"Ah, no. She's married and has a kid," he answers. "Why?"

"Just wondering."

"Just wondering if I've slept with her?" he asks. "Because the answer is hell no. I like my balls where they are, and Torin would remove them if one of us messed with his stepsister."

"Is that the only reason?" I question while my fingers fidget with the strap of my purse.

"You're cute when you're jealous," Dalton says before he grasps my chin between his finger and thumb to lift my face and kiss my lips.

It's a soft, quick kiss, but the public display of affection makes me feel a little better about where we stand after he bailed on me this morning. And since it's been bothering me, I decide to come right out and ask him about it. "What was your big rush out the door about this morning?"

Dalton's hand drops from my face at the question, then his gaze lifts to the spot above my head, like the sheriff's department is suddenly incredibly interesting.

"I knew you had an early meeting…"

"Not that early," I interrupt his bogus excuse. I reach up to hold his gorgeous face between my hands and make him look back down at me. "Just tell me the truth."

It doesn't make sense that he, the man who lives and breathes sex, would bolt when he could've gotten laid this morning. And yet, for some reason, he shows up to see me out of the blue and waits for me to come out of a meeting.

"Fine," he huffs. "My dick's broken."

"What?" I ask in confusion.

"When I didn't even have morning wood to offer, I left so that I wouldn't disappoint you again."

"Disappoint me *again*?" I repeat. "When did you disappoint me?"

"Last night," he answers. "I couldn't…we didn't…"

"You went above and beyond fulfilling any expectations I had for last night," I assure him. "I just hate that it was all one-sided. But like I told you then, it's not a big deal. Besides, sex in the mornings isn't all people do together."

"It's not?" he asks with his brow furrowed seriously, which is just freaking adorable.

"No, it's not," I respond. "There's also cuddling."

"Yeah?" Dalton asks, as if that's an entirely new notion to him. "You want to cuddle with me?"

"I'll let you in on a little secret that women keep from men," I tell him before I lower my hands from his face to rest them on his shoulders and go up on my toes to whisper in his ear, like I'm imparting some top-secret information. "Sometimes we would rather cuddle than have sex."

I feel the immediate, rigid tension in his shoulders, as if I just told him the world is about to end.

Dropping back flat on my feet to look at his blank face, I ask, "You're not a fan of cuddling?"

"I dunno," he mutters. "Never done it before."

"Yes, you have!" I assure him with a light, playful slap of my palm to his chest. "Most nights, in fact, when you let me sleep with my head on your chest and your arms around me."

"That's cuddling?" he asks.

"Pretty much. Any sort of physical contact that doesn't occur with the expectation of sexual gratification counts."

"Oh."

"So, you've probably done a lot of cuddling and never realized it," I tell him.

"I haven't, actually," he replies. "The only time women touch me is when we're in bed or they're trying to get me in bed."

"Maybe you just don't stick around long enough for the cuddling."

"Why would I stick around after we both get what we want?" he asks, not sounding the least bit angry but mostly confused.

"Because human contact without any ulterior motives or expectations is...nice," I explain. I almost ask him why he usually spends the night with me, but I'm afraid his response will be that it's easier than driving back home so late.

"There are always motives," Dalton says.

"Are there?" I ask.

"Men only stick around to cuddle because it increases their likelihood of getting laid again."

"Now that's just cynical," I tell him, even though a part of me thinks that's probably true. My ex-husband only cuddled when he was trying to get inside of me.

"Everything men and women do always goes back to sex," he

says. "We were put here to reproduce. That's it. And to make sure that happens, the act feels so good that we want to keep doing it as much as possible."

"What about love?" I ask, even though I'm not entirely sure I still believe in it.

He shakes his head. "Nothing more than a chemical reaction that results in attachment to a certain person, thanks to repeatedly having great sex with them," he answers, as if he's an expert in the field.

"That's all, huh?" I ask.

"Yep."

"Then I guess you've had a lot of women fall in love with you," I joke, since sex with Dalton is more than great. It's absolutely amazing.

"Guess so," he answers with a chuckle before he goes around and opens the driver's door for me, abruptly ending our previous topic of conversation. "So, now that your meeting is over, are you free the rest of the afternoon?"

"Looks like it."

"Good," he says. "I want to take you somewhere."

"I'm not sure if I should be worried or excited," I tell him honestly. "Is this a setup for a hit on me?"

"There is a boat involved," he says with a smile. "But I promise not to throw you overboard with a concrete block attached to your ankles."

"Wow, thanks," I scoff. "That makes me feel so much better."

"So, are you in or not?" he asks.

"In," I agree with a grin because it means spending more time with him out of bed.

"Awesome. Let's drop your SUV off at the hotel, and then we can take my bike to the docks."

"Sounds good," I agree.

CHAPTER FOURTEEN

Dalton

"Welcome to Shackleford Banks," I tell Peyton when I jump down from Sax's boat ramp with the backpack I packed for us over one shoulder. I then turn around to offer her my hand to help her.

"You brought me to a deserted island to kill me?" she asks teasingly when she joins me on the sand. Sax's head snaps around from the front of the boat in concern.

"She's joking," I tell him. "See you in three hours or so?"

"Yeah, man, see you then," he agrees before he hauls in the ramp and anchor to head back to the docks at Beaufort.

"The water here is beautiful," Peyton says.

"Yeah, it's so clear they call it the Crystal Coast," I explain to her.

After she takes off her shoes, we venture closer to the shore where the clear waves lap gently at the sand.

"Since it's a barrier island, you rarely ever get the crashing waves or riptide, unless there's a storm out in the Atlantic."

"Wow, it's so...peaceful. Where's everyone at?" she asks, glancing around the empty stretch of beach.

"It's the off season, and even during the summer not many people come out here because you need a boat to get back and forth. The ferry comes around every two hours, though, and Sax will be on standby if we need a lift before then. We won't be stuck here forever," I assure her.

I take off my shoes and roll up the cuffs of my jeans so we can get our feet wet while we walk. It may be October, but the air is still warm, with temperatures in the mid-eighties, and the water is a little crisp but refreshing.

"Do you come here often?" Peyton asks.

"Not as much lately," I answer. "My old man and I used to come camping out here for a night or two."

"Really?" she asks when she stops and turns to face me. "Does your dad live around here too?"

"Yeah," I answer.

"And you grew up here?"

Peyton suddenly makes me feel like I'm being interrogated. Still, I answer her. "No. I grew up in New York with my mom."

"So your parents split up?" she asks.

"They couldn't split up because they were never together," I explain. "My father was in his forties when he knocked up my mom, a tourist passing through town for the weekend."

"Oh," she mutters.

"I didn't see him much growing up because of the distance, but he spoiled me when I came down to visit during the summer and on holidays."

"So when did you move down here permanently? After you graduated from high school?"

"I didn't graduate," I tell her honestly. For the first time, I'm actually embarrassed by that truth. "And I didn't have a choice in relocating during the middle of my junior year of high school. My mom made me."

"Why would she make you move when you were that close to graduating?" Peyton asks.

"Because I hung out with the wrong crowd. She was a struggling Broadway dancer and she was tired of dealing with my bouts in juvie, so after I got shot, she'd had enough. She sent me down here so that my old man could try to straighten me up."

"You were shot?"

"Yeah, but it wasn't anything to do with the streets or a gang," I reply. "Not that my mom knows that."

"So then who shot you?" she asks.

Unable to lie to her, I give her the truth I've only ever told my pops. "Her best friend's husband."

Peyton

"**W**ait. Back up," I tell Dalton when he starts spilling his past to me. I'm glad he's opening up, I just wish he would slow down so I can keep up. Taking his hand, I pull him down on the sand dunes so we can sit and talk. "Your mother's best friend's husband shot you?"

"Yep."

"Why did he do that?"

"Because he found out I'd been fucking her for weeks," Dalton answers simply.

"Wow," I mutter in shock. "How old was she?"

"She was in her thirties."

"And you were..."

"I was sixteen when we started fooling around and seventeen when he caught us."

"Jesus, Dalton. Did your mother know?" I ask.

He shakes his head as he looks out at the calm water that's lapping on the shore. "Hell no. After the asshole shot me, he dragged me down and tossed me in the street where the ambulance picked me up. I guess that was better than letting me die up in his apartment."

"Where were you shot?" I ask.

Since he lost his cut before we left the hotel to set out on this adventure, Dalton whips off his white t-shirt and shows me his back. He reaches around to point to the scar that's right next to the bottom of the bearded skull. So close to his spine and vital organs.

"Oh my god," I say as I reach my fingertips out to rub over the raised scar. "You could've died."

"I almost did. And then when I didn't, they told my mom I could be paralyzed from the waist down when I woke up, depending on whether or not there was any permanent damage to my spinal cord."

"Thank goodness you were okay," I tell him.

"Yeah, I'm lucky."

"What were you...why were you sleeping with your mother's friend? A married woman?" I ask.

"I was a horny teenager. Yes, now I know it was stupid, but back then, all I cared about was that a sexy as hell woman wanted me. She was so different from the stuck-up or shy girls I went to high school with. And I thought she actually loved me like I loved her. Turned out, I was just a toy she liked to play with while her husband was at work."

"Was she your first?" I ask in concern.

"No, my third, but the first two didn't really count because they were over so fast," he replies with a chuckle. "Cora, though, well, she took her time with me for weeks, teaching me exactly how she liked things done. And then we practiced, *a lot*."

"Yuck," I say as a shiver runs through me. "I can't believe a grown woman would do that to a teenager."

"I was sixteen. It was legal."

"It may not be illegal, but that doesn't make it okay," I tell him. "You thought she cared about you?"

"I thought she was gonna leave her husband to be with me, so yeah, I thought she cared," he says. "As far as I know, they're still together. It's not like I visit often or keep in touch with my mom."

"I'm sorry," I tell him, reaching over to give his hand a squeeze.

"We never cuddled or even talked about such a thing," he says. "I never spent the night either. It was more of a drop by and drop my pants as fast as possible deal. That's why I never...I mean, even after eight years, all I know is what I did with her and women never complained."

"She was your sex education," I say in disbelief.

"Yeah, pretty much," Dalton agrees. "She was using me. But it's not like I regret it because I don't. At the time, I was fucking ecstatic that I was getting laid every day by an amazing woman when a lot of the guys I went to school with were still dreaming of being with a girl instead of their hands. I could've done without the whole getting caught and having her husband try to kill me, but it was my own damn fault. I knew she was married. I was stupid to believe Cora was really going to leave him for me when 'the time was right,'" he says, using finger quotes.

"Did you tell your father what happened when you moved down here?" I ask.

"Yeah. I had to tell someone," he answers. "I was fucking depressed as shit after losing the woman I thought I loved and having to move from the only life I had known. That's when we started working on bikes together, and he would take me camping and to the clubhouse to hang out with the guys. I think he was trying to take my mind off of everything."

"And you didn't want to go back to New York?"

"Fuck no," Dalton mutters. "There was nothing left for me there but a shitload of problems. I didn't want Cora's husband coming after me again to finish the job. And she had a chance to choose me after it all went down. Not once did she come to the hospital during the weeks I was in there."

"How did your mother not know what was going on?"

"She was working nights so when I got out of school, she was gone, and I was old enough to fend for myself. She knew I spent a lot of time at Cora's in the afternoons before I came home since she lived in the building across the street from our apartment, but she didn't know what we were doing. And I didn't want her to know. If she had found out, she would have hated Cora and made us stop seeing each other."

"But you wouldn't have been shot," I point out.

"Probably not," he agrees with a smirk.

I'm about to ask Dalton if his history with the older woman is why he's never settled down when there's a sudden snorting sound that comes from behind us. And since we're alone on the island, I jump to my feet to see where it's coming from, wishing I had brought my gun.

"Relax," Dalton says when he gets to his feet and stands next to me, looking out into the grassy dunes. "It's just the horses."

"Horses?" I ask. "There are horses on this tiny island?"

"Yeah, wild horses," he explains quietly. Then he points out two brown and white horses that are bent over and grazing, just a few hundred feet away.

"Oh wow. Look at them," I say in surprise. "How the hell did they get here?"

"I've always heard that there was a shipwreck or something hundreds of years ago and after they made it to the island, they just continued to thrive and breed."

"That's crazy," I tell him as we watch the pair. "They're beautiful."

"They don't usually get too close, but they won't run away from people either," Dalton says, gazing at the horses in awe. "My old man told me that there's only one alpha stallion allowed in a harem of mares, and that all of the other males are forced to band together and roam the island as bachelors until they're strong enough to challenge an alpha."

And when I look at Dalton, with his light hair blowing in the breeze, he reminds me of one of the wild stallion horses. He has quite a history with women, more than I imagined after what he just shared. And from everything I know, I don't think he's a man who will ever be tamed. But I can't deny that the fact that he's a savage outlaw is half of his appeal.

"Thank you for bringing me here," I whisper to him as I wind my arms around one of his and rest my head on his shoulder to enjoy the peace and serenity of the island with him. "And thank you for telling me your secrets."

"I like spending time with you," he says when he looks down at me with a smile. "How much longer are you here for?"

"Just tomorrow," I answer, even though the thought makes me kind of sad. It's nice being with Dalton during the day and not just a few hours at night.

"You're meeting with someone else tomorrow?" he asks.

"Yes."

"Will you stay here in town tomorrow night too?"

"Maybe," I reply. "If you can give me a good reason to stay."

"I think I'll be able to come up with a few," he says before he leans down and places a soft kiss on my lips and then pulls away.

The Dalton I first met a few weeks ago would have us naked and rolling around in the sand by now. But I'm starting to think I like this Dalton, the one who brings me to a private island and tells me about his history, even better.

CHAPTER FIFTEEN

Dalton

After we catch a ride with Sax off the island, I take Peyton to a little burger shop on the pier to eat dinner and then we head back to her hotel room.

Is it weird that I'm nervous that tonight will be a repeat performance of last night when I couldn't perform?

I mean, I definitely want to be with Peyton. So hopefully the rest of my body agrees.

Instead of undressing and heading straight to bed, she thankfully opens up the sliding glass door that reveals the ocean, letting in the breeze as the sun starts to set.

Standing behind her as we silently take it all in, I wrap my arms around Peyton's waist and rest my chin on the top of her head.

"I'm meeting with the chief of the Wilmington Police Department tomorrow about the Ace of Spades bar that burned down a year ago," she eventually says while we continue to watch the waves breaking on the shore.

"Oh yeah?" I ask, even though I'm not all that surprised.

"Anything I should know going in, like he's related to someone in the Savage Kings?"

"Not that I know of," I tell her truthfully. "Wasn't that, like, a gas line or a meth lab that exploded?" I hedge since I know damn well why it went up in flames because I was there.

"So I've heard," Peyton replies. "I'll see what the reports say."

"Yeah."

"If the Savage Kings go down and you're the one in charge of laundering money, you would probably get the longest prison sentence," Peyton says frankly.

"Then it's a good thing we're not involved in any illegal shit, right?" I reply, even though the thought of going to prison scares the piss out of me. It's a miracle I've made it to twenty-five and never spent more than a night inside for questioning.

Turning around in my arms to look up at my face, Peyton says, "I don't want to be the one responsible for sending you away."

"That's not gonna happen," I tell her.

"If I find something in Wilmington tomorrow, I can't ignore it just because we're sleeping together."

"There's nothing to find," I respond, even though I wish I could be completely honest with her and that she could overlook whatever the club has done because she cares about me.

"Well, if that's true, then my job here in the Eastern District will be over soon, and I'll be heading back to Georgia."

"So, the only way you get to stick around is if you bring charges against the MC?" I ask in understanding. My chest tightens at the idea of Peyton leaving the state for good. And I'm not sure which is worse, not seeing her again or thinking about the MC that my old man not only helped form but loved more than life going down. Or my brothers who have become my second family having to serve long prison sentences.

"I'm sorry," Peyton says into the long, drawn-out silence.

"Nothing to do about it tonight, right?" I ask, reaching for the hem of her shirt and pulling it up over her head.

"Dalton! The sliding door is still open!" she chastises me when I get to work on her pants.

"So?" I reply. "If I only know one thing about you, it's that you get turned on at the idea of being on display. Besides, the Kings still own this town, at least for one more night. May as well make the most of it," I tell her before I lower my lips to hers, trying to kiss away whatever the future holds, at least until the sun comes up tomorrow.

Peyton

"Thanks for meeting with me," I tell the Wilmington PD Chief of Police.

"Not a problem," Chief Adkins says. "I made you copies of all our files." He hands me a stack of folders about three inches thick from across the desk. It's so heavy my arm sags with their weight.

"This is all the Savage Kings?" I ask in dismay.

"Yes, ma'am," he agrees, clasping his fingers on top of his desk. "No arrests came from any of it, though. The long and the short is, there was a fire at a rival MC's bar and then a shooting on the highway. The fire was ruled an accident because there was a meth lab in a trailer behind it that exploded, killing the president of the Ace of Spades MC."

"Wow." I let that sink in for a second. "And what about the shooting on the highway?" I ask since I don't have any information on that.

"One dead, two seriously injured, all three with connections to Hector Cruz who..."

"Was also killed in a shootout," I finish for him since I know that much.

"Yes," the chief replies.

"So why did you think it was the Savage Kings on the highway?"

"An eyewitness recognized the bearded skull king logo on the leather jacket that the rider had on. But we didn't have enough evidence to bring the whole crew in for a line-up."

"Oh," I mutter, knowing from experience that the logo is one you don't forget.

"Then the highway patrol officer who was investigating the case died just a few days later..."

"What?" I exclaim.

"It *looked* like an accidental drowning, and there was nothing else to point to any foul play, so the case pretty much just fizzled out."

"Looked like an accidental drowning?" I repeat in concern.

"These MC guys are smart. They're careful not to leave any evidence. Besides, rumors surfaced after the trooper's death. No one likes to paint a dead officer in a bad light, so we didn't investigate for his family's sake, but I've heard the trooper also had ties to Hector Cruz..."

"Three separate deaths—eight, if you count Hector and the four other men found dead at his crime scene—all with Cruz connections and signs pointing at the Savage Kings having motive?"

"Sounds like more than a coincidence, doesn't it?" the chief asks. "But only two out of those four incidents occurred in my jurisdiction. The rest were in Carteret, where the Kings allegedly control the law enforcement."

"The sheriff is the stepsister of the Savage Kings' president and VP."

"Exactly," he agrees. "Maybe you'll have more luck than we did putting the puzzle pieces all together with the federal jurisdiction. But between you and me, I have to live here, and I have a family. The Savage Kings MC is not the group of men I want to piss off personally."

"Right," I agree.

Should I be worried about the MC doing something to me if I keep investigating? Dalton seemed a little concerned about someone in the club "fucking with me" while I was in town. I feel certain that Dalton would never harm me in any way, but could I say the same for his friends that are more than likely connected to not one, but *eight* deaths in the area in a little over a year?

No, I can't.

These guys live by their own code, one where brotherhood is more important than any other relationship.

So, if it came down to it, and Dalton had to choose sides, I have no doubt he would choose the MC over me.

CHAPTER SIXTEEN

Dalton

All day today, ever since I left Peyton's hotel room, I've had this sense of impending doom, like there's a guillotine blade hanging over my head, ready to fall at any second.

I'm sure it's just my concern about what Peyton found out when she met with the Wilmington PD, and whether or not she'll try to convince the U.S. Attorney to drop the investigation against the Savage Kings.

But when she opens her hotel room door, I know right away it's not good news, based on the way her eyes immediately lower from mine.

"Hey," I say in greeting.

"Hey," she replies.

"Can I come in?" I ask when she doesn't step aside to allow me entry.

"Yeah," she agrees, but it's definitely not the enthusiastic welcome I usually get from her when I show up to her house every night. Most of the time, she practically jumps on me before I get her to her bedroom.

"You okay?" I ask after she shuts the hotel door.

"Those are the files the Wilmington PD gave me today," Peyton says with a nod toward the stack of documents on the small round hotel table near the kitchen.

Shit.

"Mind if I take a look?" I ask her.

"Go for it."

Heading over, I sit down in one of the two chairs and start reading the first page. It takes me an hour to get through all of the various documents, none of which paint the MC in a very favorable light.

"Have you read it all yet?" I lean back in my chair and ask Peyton, who has been quietly watching the television from her seat on the foot of the bed while I was reading.

"Yes," she answers without looking at me.

"And?"

"And that's a lot of dead bodies, Dalton," she replies.

"It's not as bad as it looks..."

"Oh really?" she asks, now turning her sad eyes to me. "Eight people died in the span of a few months, and the only suspects were the Savage Kings."

"If that were true, then why haven't any of us been arrested?" I ask.

"Because the sheriff doesn't give a shit and the police chief is scared of you!"

"Did you ever consider that the people who died were horrible human beings?"

"No, you don't get to pull the whole *world is a better place* bullshit. If they were the bad guys, then they deserved to be locked up, not dead!"

"Why are you yelling at me?" I ask. "I didn't kill anyone."

"But the people you know, the ones you call brothers, *did* kill people, didn't they?"

"That's not a question I can answer, and you know it," I point out.

"Will they kill me if I don't drop the investigation?"

"What the hell kind of question is that?" I scoff. "The Savage Kings don't go around hurting women."

"Maybe not," Peyton replies. "But I don't feel comfortable letting anyone get away with killing men without any consequences."

"And who do you think killed someone?"

"I don't know! But if I keep digging, I think I could figure it out!" she throws her hands up and exclaims.

"Look." I get up and go over to kneel between her legs, grabbing her hands. "I'm not asking you to give the Savage Kings a break because you and I are sleeping together. But I wish you would give us the benefit of the doubt and let the shit in the past go because you know how important the MC is to me."

My plea doesn't work. That much is obvious when Peyton refuses to meet my eyes.

"Maybe...maybe I should go home tomorrow, and we should stop seeing each other."

Fuck.

Part of me wants to yell and scream at her that we should just end things fucking now, and then storm right out the door.

But that's only a knee-jerk reaction for feeling hurt because she doesn't think I'm worth the risks associated with having a relationship with an outlaw. Sure, it would temporarily feel like I have the upper hand to run out on her, but it'll suck to not get to spend one last night with her.

So instead of raising hell, I simply say, "Okay. I'll stay tonight and then you can leave tomorrow, and hopefully never think about the Savage Kings again."

"Yeah," she agrees with a nod.

Knowing this is it, a few more hours with Peyton is all I'll get, I don't want to waste any more time. I need to hold her and kiss her, and be inside of her as many times as she'll let me. Getting to my feet, I lean down and press my lips to hers several times until she parts them to let my tongue ease inside. I want to show her just how much I'm gonna miss her. Hell, maybe all she'll miss of me is the sex, and if so, then I want to give her a lot of great memories tonight.

Too bad that right after I've managed to ride her down to the mattress, my fucking phone starts ringing.

"Do you need to get that?" Peyton pulls back from our kiss to ask.

I yank the personal phone out of my pocket, intending to ignore the caller until I see the name of the contact on the screen. "Shit," I mutter. "Sorry, but I should probably answer..."

"Yeah, sure," she agrees with a nod.

"Hello?" I say after I press the button to answer and sit up, straddling Peyton's waist.

"This is Anita from *Morningview Nursing Home*. I hate to bother you so late, but your number is listed as the emergency contact for Rubin Brady."

"Yeah, I know. I'm his son. What's wrong?" I ask in concern since they don't usually call at night when it's about his basic routine care.

"Well, Mr. Brady is suddenly very intent on leaving the premises. Our night staff is doing all they can to restrain him but he's persistent. We thought perhaps a familiar face may help to get him back to his room."

"Okay, yeah, I'm on my way," I say before I end the call.

"Everything okay?" Peyton asks.

"No," I reply with a heavy exhale when I climb off of her. "I'm really sorry, but I have to go." And fuck, I wanted to stay here with her every second of her last night. Now I don't know how long I'll be gone.

"Go where?" she questions.

"This is not how I wanted our last night to go," I assure her. "But I don't know how long it'll take..."

"Dalton, what is it?" she asks again, getting to her feet and resting her hand on my bicep reassuringly. "Where are you going? I'll come with you."

"No, you should stay here," I say with a shake of my head as I start toward the door.

"Is it...is it club business?" she questions.

"No," I answer. "It's nothing to do with the club."

"Then I'm coming with you," she declares.

I look at her for several long seconds, before I eventually cave because I don't want to lose a second with her tonight. "Are you sure? This isn't gonna be fun."

"I can handle it."

"Fine," I reply. "But we need to hurry."

Peyton

I'm riding on the back of Dalton's bike with my arms around his waist for only the second time. Unlike the trip to the docks, this ride is much faster and a little scary as he races to get to wherever we're going. Since I only heard his side of the phone conversation, I have no idea where that is, only that it must have something to do with his father.

Pulling into the *Morningview Nursing Home* was the last place I imagined we were headed. Before we even get off the bike, I spot the tall, white-haired man with a long, Santa beard at the gate. He's wearing what looks like a black Savage Kings leather cut with his jeans and is heading our way despite the fact that there's a woman hanging off each of his thick arms, trying to slow him down. They're obviously not having any luck since he's built like a linebacker.

"Fuck," Dalton mutters as we take off and hang our helmets on the bike's handlebars. "Meet my father, Rubin," he says to me, his jaw clenched tight. "He has advanced Alzheimer's and the ankle bracelet they put on him only notifies them when he leaves the building, but they can't actually stop him once he gets something on his mind."

"Jeez. I'm so sorry," I tell him, taking his hand and linking our fingers together as we start heading toward the group.

"Where do you think you're going, Pop?" Dalton asks when we're only a few feet away. "You need to get back inside."

Finally, the white-haired man pulls up short, looking from his son to the motorcycle and back again, his handsome face scrunched in confusion.

"Who the hell are you?" he roars. "What the fuck are you doing on my bike? That's my goddamn Knucklehead!" He then lurches for Dalton, his arm arching like he's going to punch him. The women are, of course, unable to stop his momentum. Luckily though, his movements are slow, so Dalton releases my hand, pushes me behind him, and is still able to dodge his fist. He then wraps his arms around his father's shoulders in a restraining hug to prevent him from taking another swing, even though the older man continues to flail, trying to get away.

"Calm down! It's okay," Dalton assures him in a rush. "You're right. That *is* your bike. It needed a new carburetor, so I took it to my shop to repair it for you."

"Oh," his father says, and finally stops fighting him. "You fixed it?"

"Yeah, old man. I fixed it."

Since he seems to be calming down, Dalton releases his hold on him and takes a step back.

His father squints his eyes down at him and says, "Deacon? Deacon, is that you? Where have you been, you son of a bitch?" He wraps Dalton in a crushing hug and calls him someone else's name like he's a long-lost friend. My heart breaks knowing that because of the dementia, he doesn't even recognize his own son. I can't imagine how difficult that must be for Dalton...

Gaze zeroing in on me, his father, Rubin, asks, "And who is this pretty young thing?" Dalton looks over his shoulder at me, and before he can reply, his dad chuckles and says, "You old dog! You finally went and got yourself an old lady, huh?"

"No, P—" Dalton catches himself before he calls him Pop. "No, Rubin. She's not my old lady. This is my...friend, Peyton."

"Peyton?" Rubin repeats my name several times. "I don't know any Peytons. I think...I think I may know a...a Dalton, though."

"Yeah, you do," Dalton replies with a sigh. "He's your son."

"Son? No, I don't have any kids," he responds swiftly, like he's certain of that fact.

God, I feel so bad for Dalton. He told me yesterday that he doesn't have a relationship with his mother, but it sounded like he grew close to his father after he moved down here to North Carolina. Now, though, he doesn't even have that relationship since his father doesn't remember him.

"Why don't we go back inside so we can sit down and catch up," Dalton suggests, taking Rubin's elbow and spinning him back around toward the nursing home.

"Yeah, yeah, okay," he eventually agrees. "But I can't wait to go for a ride on my bike again. It's been too long. So long...well, I don't even remember."

"Maybe another day. A thunderstorm's coming up tonight," Dalton tells him as he ushers him into the building and down a hall, past a nurse's station.

"Is it now?" Rubin asks. "Guess we better hunker down here for a while."

His living area is larger than a standard hospital room and holds more comforts, like a sitting area with a loveseat and recliner, and personal belongings consisting of photographs of motorcycles, some with scantily-dressed women in bikinis.

"Take a load off and catch me up," Rubin tells us, so Dalton and I sit next to each other on the little sofa while Rubin lounges in his chair. "How's the MC project going? You got any charters going in Virginia or South Carolina?"

"Yeah," Dalton answers. "Four in South and five in Virginia."

"No shit? Nine new ones?" Rubin responds, sounding impressed. "You've come a long way from our one little shithole bar."

"Every man who owns a Harley on the East Coast wants to be a Savage King," Dalton says with a smile.

"Damn right they do," his father says with a thumb of his right fist to the patch on the left side of his vest. "I told you they would. You're giving them something they need in their life, just like you gave me when I was down on my luck without a penny to my name—a sense of pride and a place to call home; brothers who are there through thick and thin, no matter what."

"What was it you called the clubhouse again? A halfway house for crooks and vets with one foot in the black and another in the grave?" Dalton prompts him.

"You can save them all by getting both of their feet on the footpegs of a Harley. Once they start riding, they'll never want to get off."

"Yeah, you can," Dalton agrees before he reaches over and covers the hand that's resting on my thigh with his to give it a squeeze.

And I know that his touch isn't just for comfort, even though I'm guessing he needs a little of that too right now, dealing with his sick father. But I also understand that he wants me to listen and understand what the MC is all about. It's not the crimes that define them but the cohesiveness of the brotherhood.

CHAPTER SEVENTEEN

Dalton

"I'm really sorry he got out of control tonight," I tell the two women at the nurses' station a few hours later, when Peyton and I are finally able to get my dad in bed for the night.

"No, we're sorry we had to call you in so late," one of them replies. "We can usually talk the dementia patients down, but Rubin's a big man and we don't have any male attendings working tonight."

"Yeah, he's big and stubborn," I agree with a smile.

"As soon as he has another good day, we're gonna move him upstairs to the second floor, where the stairways and elevators have a code," she assures me.

"That would be great, thanks," I tell her. "Have a good night."

"You too," they say before Peyton and I walk out the nursing home's front door.

"Sorry our last night got ruined," I tell her on the way back to my bike.

"It's okay," she says to me, linking her hands in the crook of my arm. "That must be tough to handle when he doesn't recognize you..."

"Half the time when I visit, he thinks I'm Deacon, his best friend who died six years ago from lung cancer. Apparently, I look like Chase and Torin's uncle when he was younger," I tell her. "When the dementia first started, I would argue until I was blue in the face that I was Dalton, his goddamn son. But then I realized it was futile. Trying to convince him made the bad days even worse. And how can I be mad at him because his mind is deteriorating? It's not like he did this on purpose."

Stabbing my fingers through my hair and blowing out a breath of frustration, I say, "Now I always just roll with being Deacon because mistaking me as an old friend is better than him not recognizing me at all and yelling at me to get the fuck out of his room."

"Yeah," Peyton agrees, and I can feel her sympathetic gaze. "And it's pretty cool to hear about those stories from the MC. Did he tell you them before?"

"Nope," I answer. "I like hearing about him and all their friends. But once he starts talking about the good ole days, he doesn't stop for a long time." Since she may not know the club's history, I tell her, "Deacon started the Savage Kings MC for military vets and convicts down on their luck on the fringes of society. He wanted them to form a brotherhood to help keep each other out of trouble and out of the ground. And it worked. Mostly."

"Sounds like he and your father had really good intentions," she replies.

"Well, they also wanted the town to become a biker's paradise, like Bike Week at Myrtle Beach, only all Harleys and babes in bikinis all summer long," I tell her with a grin.

"So what if they were not completely altruistic," she teases when we reach my bike. "And after meeting your father, I'm starting to see that the handsome, big talker thing must be genetic."

"Guess so," I agree, my smile widening because I enjoy her pointing out the similarities between me and my old man. "When I first moved here, I didn't think he and I had anything in common," I explain. "I mean, he was almost sixty when I was only seventeen. But he was genuinely happy to have me around and eventually, we bonded over bikes and the MC."

"How long has he been like this?" she asks with a nod of her head toward the nursing home.

"About three years," I reply. "He was forgetting shit all the time before that. But then, after he lost Deacon, he started getting worse, like not remembering he was gone. When he forgot things, he got angry, mostly at himself. I took his keys and hid them, but he'd leave the house on foot and wander for miles. That's when I knew it was time to get him around-the-clock care to make sure he stayed safe. Sometimes he's just too big and stubborn for them to handle."

"You don't have any brothers or sisters to help you?" she asks.

Flashing her a grin, I say, "None that I know about. My dad may not *think* he has any other kids, but he was a ladies' man, so there are probably brothers and sisters from his glory days out in the world."

"So that's where you get your charm from too," Peyton says.

"Must be," I agree, even though I feel like whenever I'm around her, she zaps up all of my charisma that works on other women but not her. With Peyton, I'm not much better than a fumbling teenager on his first date. Not that I've ever really had many dates, so I guess that explains why I'm so out of my element.

"It's getting late. I should probably get you back to the hotel," I tell her.

"Right," she agrees before climbing on the back of my bike.

On the drive back to the *Jolly Roger*, I wonder about what the nursing home would have done if I had been in Raleigh with her when my old man decided he was going to leave. I need to stay closer, which sucks because that's just another reason why Peyton and I need to end this for good. That's pretty damn hard when I crave more and more time with her.

I park my bike in front of the hotel lobby and kill the engine, but don't climb off.

"Aren't you coming in?" Peyton asks when she gets off the back and hands me her helmet.

"I don't know," I answer honestly. "Maybe...maybe we should just go ahead and say our goodbyes now because if I take you to bed tonight, I'm not gonna want to leave in the morning."

"Please come up?" she begs, taking my hand in hers. "I'm not ready to say goodbye to you just yet."

Pulling my phone from my jeans pocket, I check to see if there are any missed calls from the nursing home while we were riding. If so, that'll be a great excuse to not have to go up to her room tonight and leave tomorrow feeling like my chest has been ripped open. There are no missed calls or messages. By now, the nurses have probably given Rubin his meds to knock him out for the night, so I guess that excuse won't work, since I'm not going to let a lie be the last thing I say to Peyton.

"Looks like everything's calmed down back at the nursing home so, yeah, I'll come in," I tell her.

"Good," she says on an exhale. "I'll wait here while you go park."

Nodding my agreement, I let her hand go and kickstart the engine to pull around to the first empty parking space I find. On the walk back to Peyton, I try to give myself a pep talk about not being a pussy. I just need to fuck her tonight like any other woman, and then get the hell out of there.

But Peyton's not like anyone else.

And maybe I'm a sadist because, no matter how hard it will be to let her leave tomorrow morning, knowing she'll never come back, I want every last second I can get with her, even the cuddling.

Peyton

I'm starting to realize Dalton is looking forward to the end of our time together about as much as I am.

Did he really think I would let him just drop me off and ride away tonight?

No fucking way.

I want to kiss every inch of him one last time. I want to soak up the feeling of his warm, hard body pressed against mine while he's inside me. And then I want to fall asleep with his strong arms wrapped tightly around me, like he doesn't plan to ever let go, even if we both know he will in a few hours.

While being with Dalton is amazing, I can't keep risking my career, my livelihood, on a man I just met, especially one who is more than likely going to break my heart when he ends up falling in bed with someone else. It's what he does.

"Ready?" I ask with as much of a smile as I can muster when Dalton strolls up to me outside the hotel after parking his bike.

"Yeah," he agrees, taking my hand, and we head inside to the elevator bank.

The ride up to my room is silent because Dalton is unusually quiet. The fact that he's not joking and teasing me with his smart mouth is a little worrisome. I'm even a little nervous as I unlock the door and we step inside the room. More nervous than I was the first night with Henry, the man who was too gorgeous and perfect to be real.

Now that I've gotten to know Dalton, I'm well aware he has flaws, yet none of that deters me from still wanting him more than anything else in the world right now.

I go over and turn on both lamps on either side of the bed because I want to see and remember everything we're about to do. Then I start to wonder if Dalton even wants to have sex. He's had an emotional night dealing with his father. That's why, when I walk up and stand in front of him, I ask, "Do you want to just get in bed and cuddle tonight?"

"No," he answers without delay, and part of me is relieved he still wants me.

His hands come up and get to work unbuttoning my blouse. After I step out of my shoes, Dalton meticulously removes my jeans, then my bra and panties, until I'm standing in front of him naked while he looks at me but doesn't touch.

"Your turn," I tell him, reaching for his cut when my self-consciousness can't take being silently stared at any longer.

"Hold on," he says, removing both of my hands from his cut and holding them while his eyes continue to roam over me from head to toe. "I'm trying to memorize every beautiful curve on your body. And once I strip down, I won't be able to just look anymore."

"Take a picture. It'll last longer," I tell him, and I'm not sure who is more surprised by my offer, me or him.

"Really?" Dalton asks with both eyebrows raised.

"Just remember that I know where you live if you upload them to some sleezy website," I joke. He grins like a kid in a candy store before he quickly retrieves one of his phones and snaps a photo of my face and then steps back to get a full frontal.

"Turn around," he says.

"Seriously?" I ask.

He simply makes the twirling gesture with his finger without saying another word, so I eventually comply, even going so far as to brace my hands on the nightstand to really push out my ass. It's a pose that I would never have considered doing for a man before I met Dalton.

"Fucking perfect," he says from behind me before I hear the snap of the photo on his old untraceable flip phone. I try not to think too hard about why he has two phones.

From the corner of my eye, I see the phone go flying, landing on the mattress, before Dalton's tall shadow descends on me. He pushes my hair aside from my right shoulder so that his lips can place a kiss on my skin. His hands come down on my hips as he fits the front of his clothed body to my backside and says, "Now I'll always have a photo to remind me of that first night when you were bent over the backseat for me."

A shiver runs down my spine while a boulder lodges in my throat when I realize that I don't have a photo or anything else to remember Dalton by. Just memories that will eventually fade once I'm back in Georgia, until I can't even remember all of the details of his face.

But when one of Dalton's hands lower and cup me so possessively, so familiarly between my legs while his lips pick up the pace and starts kissing my neck, the time for thinking is over. I close my eyes so I can just focus on feeling everywhere he's touching me, especially that warmth spreading in my chest that only he's capable of reaching.

CHAPTER EIGHTEEN

Dalton

"Are you awake?" I slide my hand up Peyton's stomach and ask from behind her when I wake up after our last hot and heavy round, needing her yet again. First, I had her when she was naked and bent over when I was still fully-clothed. Then, she made quick work of getting me undressed and went down on me before riding me hard and fast. But hearing her scream my name twice wasn't nearly enough.

"Yes," she answers softly before she rolls to her back so I can mount her. Our mouths collide into a searing, hot kiss as I devour her while my hand feels around the bedside table for a condom.

When I sit back on my knees to roll it on, Peyton asks, "Is that your last one?"

"Yeah," I answer. "Guess I better make it count."

"I'm sure you will," she replies with a small smile, her blonde hair spread out around her and practically glowing, thanks to the soft light of the lamps in the otherwise dark room.

"Come here," I say, grabbing Peyton's hips and pulling her onto my lap. I ease her down on my cock as she wraps her arms around my neck and locks her legs behind my back. We're face-to-face, chest to chest, while I'm inside of her. From this position, I can easily kiss her while I run my hands through her hair and hold her as our bodies stay connected, moving in synchrony.

"You feel so good," she whispers against my lips as her breath begins to stagger, telling me she's already getting close.

"Not yet," I say when I pull her off my shaft to make sure she doesn't come so soon because as soon as she does, it's all over for me, then it's all over for us.

"Please, Dalton," Peyton begs as she wiggles her hips and tries to climb on me again.

"Delayed gratification," I remind her, even though I'm in agony myself.

For the next few minutes, she pulls my hair and claws my back as I kiss her and keep her from coming apart, even though she's dying to.

"Ugh, I won't miss you being a withholding asshole," she huffs when she finally has enough and starts to push me away to climb off of me.

"Sure, you will," I tell her when I tackle her down on the mattress, so she's flat on her back.

"Maybe a little," she agrees softly as she holds my face in her hands and stares up at me. "But only if you kiss me and finally make love to me."

"I was trying to make it last," I explain to her.

"I know," Peyton agrees as she reaches down between us and lines up my cock to enter her. "Now just make it good."

With that request, I sink inside of her and then savor each second that our bodies are joined while looking down into her eyes. In them, I see everything that I'm feeling reflected right back at me.

"I'm close," Peyton eventually says.

"I know, kitten," I tell her. "Me too."

"Don't stop," she pants.

And fuck, I don't want to stop. Ever.

Why is it that the one woman I'm actually starting to fall for is a goddamn ATF agent who lives in another state? I would give anything to change both of those things. But I can't. Just like I can't change my past or give my dad his memories back. Some things are out of my control and I can't fucking stand it.

So, I decide to take back control of what I can.

And instead of giving Peyton the sweet ending she wants, I flip her body over and slam into her from behind. Hell, to really piss her off, I grab a handful of her hair and give it a tug while I pound her into the mattress.

"Why?" Peyton looks over her shoulder and asks, or she tries to before I jerk on her hair. I don't want to see the disappointment on her face.

"Because I can," I tell her.

She calls me several horrible names before her pussy clamps down on my cock. She comes so hard she milks me dry while crying out my actual name.

I haven't even caught my breath when she says, "Get the fuck out."

Unlike the afternoon in her townhouse, I know she means every word this time. She wants me gone, out of her life for good.

It's better this way, leaving with her face down, naked on the bed and angry at me, instead of me breaking down and begging her to stay with me in the morning, after hours of cuddling, right? I won't lower myself to acting like a goddamn pussy just to convince her that we're good together or could figure out a way to make this work.

But as I climb off the bed to throw the condom away in the bathroom and get dressed, I start to think maybe I've made a mistake. A huge one I'll regret for the rest of my life.

Peyton

Damn him!

Why did Dalton have to go and ruin our last time together?

There were so many amazing moments with him over the last few weeks, and now they're all overshadowed by the one time Dalton was a jerk.

As soon as he moved on top of me the final time, things changed. I felt it, and so I'm sure he did too. What had been casual between us suddenly became more...

I think that's why Dalton was trying to piss me off, to stop the sudden onset of feelings. It definitely worked. I wanted him gone, too angry and hurt to even look at him.

But as soon as the hotel door clicks shut with his departure, I want to beg him to come back.

That seems to be the effect he has on me. I shouldn't want to be with him, yet for weeks, I couldn't resist.

And now...now, things are over. For good. That's the last time I'll ever have to see the back of his stupid leather cut with that damn bearded skull wearing a crown.

This is a good thing, how we both knew it would end.

So why does it feel like my heart is being ripped from my chest?

It was just sex, right?

Until it wasn't.

CHAPTER NINETEEN

Dalton

"Any other business we need to discuss?" Torin asks as we all sit around the Savage Kings table and start winding up our meeting.

My body may be present, but my head and heart are still back in the hotel room, remembering every second of my last night with Peyton.

It's only been a week, yet I couldn't tell you how many times I've gone east on Highway 40 to see her, only to turn around and head home with my tail between my legs. Now I'm certain that I'm acting like a pussy because I can't stop thinking about her, though I know we're both better off apart. After how I left her, odds are she would shoot me rather than invite me in.

And soon the club will find out if she's decided to bring us down. If not, it's back to Georgia for Peyton...

"Yeah, one more thing," Sax, our club's secretary, speaks up and says. "Dalton, what the hell have you been doing over in Raleigh?"

Startling out of my pensiveness at the sound of my name, I say, "How did you know I—"

"Some guys in their charter have spotted you riding down 40 on your one in a million bike, wearing your cut, several times over the last few weeks," Sax grumbles.

"So? Why the fuck do they care if I'm there?" I ask defensively, more grumpy than usual without being able to see Peyton. "It's none of their fucking business."

"Because you're an officer in the *original* Savage Kings charter," Sax reminds me. "They called because they thought they had fucked up and that you were there on club business to keep an eye on them."

"Wow. They're big damn pussies over in Raleigh," I grumble. "I didn't know the *original* Kings had to ask for permission to travel outside our city limits."

"You're right," Torin says. "You don't have to ask for permission or ride in a group everywhere you go, but you're asking for trouble riding that far alone."

"The ATF agent lives in Raleigh," Reece pipes up and outs me from across the table, making me curse under my breath.

"An ATF agent?" Coop repeats. "The one we stole the goddamn laptop from?"

"That would be the one," Reece answers with a grin that I want to punch off of his face. "Peyton Bradley."

"You're not that fucking stupid, are you?" Chase asks me with a scowl.

"We're just fucking. We *were* just fucking," I amend. "It's over and done now. I swear."

"No," Torin says, rubbing his chin in thought.

"Excuse me?" I ask him.

"Keep seeing her," Torin says.

"What the hell?" Chase asks. "She's a fed who's investigating us! For all we know, she could be using him to get dirt on the damn club!"

Isn't that exactly what I thought too? Now, I'm not so sure.

"All she was using was my dick," I snap at our VP in Peyton's defense, which I admit, doesn't sound all that much better, but I don't think she was just sleeping with me to get details. Hopefully.

"Dalton isn't stupid," Torin argues, then narrows his eyes at me before he adds, "Most of the time. We know he'll keep his mouth shut about club business, so if he thinks he has this shit under control then he should, you know, keep seeing her."

"Ah, thanks for the vote of confidence there, Pres," I mutter. "But seeing her again is not an option."

"Why not? You lost your powers? No more panties drop wherever you happen to appear?" Abe teases.

"No, but..."

"Then keep fucking her," Torin says. "We have Jade watching our backs as the Sheriff on the state level, but we could use a federal ally."

As Chase and Torin's stepsister, she's family, so she owes them some loyalty. Peyton would never back the MC. But would she cover for me if it came to it? Maybe.

"I can't guarantee she'll ever have our backs despite how amazing I am in the sack," I tell him.

Rolling his eyes, Torin says, "That's a chance I think we'll be willing to take."

"So, you want me to use her?" I ask for clarification.

"No," Torin answers, lifting the corner of his lips. "We want *her* to keep using *you*."

Shaking my head in disbelief, I tell him, "That's just wrong, Pres."

"Does anyone feel bad for Dalton taking one for the club? Or think the risks outweigh the benefits?" Torin asks the men gathered around the table. "Let's vote it. All in favor of Dalton whoring himself out for the club?"

"Nay!" I huff.

Yea is spoken in unison by ten assholes and Abe feels the need to add, "When has Dalton *not* been whoring himself out? At least now it will be for a good reason."

Some of the guys chuckle while a smirking Torin slams down his gavel on the table ceremoniously and says, "Looks like it passes almost unanimously."

"Fuck you all," I tell them as I wave both of my middle fingers in front of my face at them when everyone pushes their chairs back and starts to leave the chapel.

So now I have the MC's blessing on seeing Peyton. The question is, how the hell do I convince her that she should keep seeing me after the way I treated her the last night we were together, and when we live so far apart?

CHAPTER TWENTY

Peyton

"Your phone's ringing. Again," Quincey says as we sip martinis at the bar after work.

"Yep," I mutter but I don't answer it. Instead, Quincey grabs it from my purse.

"Unknown," she reads from the screen.

"Yep."

"Your gorgeous bad boy is still calling?" she asks. "How long has it been now? Two weeks?"

"Three," I correct.

"Wow. Three weeks and you're still refusing to talk to him?" she replies. "You must have the willpower of a nun."

"He's also been sending flowers," I tell her while trying to keep my facial expression neutral. It's harder than I expect, thinking about the beautiful, colorful bouquets made with a variety of flowers.

"Oh really?" Quincey asks with a grin. "What kind?"

"All sorts, he mixes it up each day," I tell her, barely concealing my grin as I also recall all of the sweet notes. The ones I love the best say that he hasn't been with anyone else and he'll remain celibate for the rest of his life unless he gets to be with me. Do I believe that for an instant? No, but he does know exactly what I want to hear.

"Oh my god. Now you're just being downright cruel to the man," Quincey huffs.

"No matter how much I want to see him again, what's the point? We could never work since we're living two very different lives. And he lives two hours away now. If I throw in the towel on the investigation, it'll be even farther once I'm back in Georgia."

"Are you going to recommend that the U.S. Attorney drop the investigation?" she asks.

"I haven't decided yet."

"Of course you are," she replies. "You're just stalling. And a two-hour drive is all there is right now, which is nothing," she says with a wave of her hand. "Come on, let's get in the car and head to the coast tonight. I'll go with you! He has hot biker friends, right?"

"You think I should drive two hours on a Friday night to go see Dalton with another woman?" I ask. "No, thanks."

"If you saw him with another woman, would you finally stop moping around like a sick puppy all the time?"

"I'm already angry with him," I tell her. Not that I've gone into details about him ruining our final night together by being an asshole. "If I go and see him with another woman, it's possible I may chop his dick off."

"If he didn't have a dick, I bet you could get over him," Quincey points out. And even I can admit there's some logic to that notion.

"Fine," I say with a heavy sigh. "Let's go to the beach."

"Really?" she asks with a near supersonic squeal.

"Yes. But if this ends horribly, I'm going to blame it all on you."

Three hours later, and we're parking my SUV on the strip about three blocks away from the Savage Kings' clubhouse because the whole street around the hotel and bar is slam packed with cars and Harleys.

"What do you think is going on?" Quincey asks as we get out and start walking back to the bustling area.

"No clue."

"Whatever it is, it looks like it's drawing a big crowd," she says. "Which means we should be able to blend right in."

"Let's go in the bar first and see what we can find out," I suggest.

The *Savage Asylum* parking lot is completely full, but when we go inside, there's not a single person in the room. At least not at first.

"Oh shit," I mutter when I spot a big, intimidating man I recognize from his military photo in the case file—Torin Fury, the Savage Kings' president. The only thing that makes him a little less frightening is the tiny baby dressed all in pink that's currently sleeping on the shoulder of his leather cut.

Narrowing his eyes at me and Quincey, he softly asks, "What are you doing here?"

Crap. Does he recognize me? I'm guessing so. If I had to bet, he would've yelled those words with a few expletives if not for the sleeping infant.

"I was...we were looking for Dalton," I answer.

"Is that it?" he asks with an arched eyebrow, and I know he's really asking if I'm there to arrest anyone.

"Yes."

"He's at the fight," he informs us.

"Fight?" I repeat.

"MMA fight across the street in our new outdoor arena," he says, nodding to the poster on the wall behind us, depicting two buff guys posing with their gloves raised in the air.

"Oh."

"Can I give you some advice?" Torin asks as he gently adjusts the baby on his shoulder.

"Ah, sure," I answer.

"Stay the hell away from the Savage Kings."

"I am," I tell him. "The investigation is done. I just have to send the report to the U.S. Attorney."

Guess Quincey was right, and my decision has already been made.

"Good," Torin says. "Head toward the beach and you'll see the spotlights."

"Thanks," I reply as I start to turn to leave, ready to get out from under his wrathful gaze.

"The MC is a part of him," Torin suddenly says, making me stop in my tracks to look back over my shoulder at him. "It's not just a cut he wears, or the ink on his skin. It's in his blood and always will be. The sooner you realize that, the better off you'll be."

"I know that," I mutter. "The MC isn't the problem."

"Then what is?" Torin asks.

When I hesitate with my response, Quincey answers for me. "She's worried he'll cheat on her like her ex-husband."

Torin chuckles at that. "Dalton *was* a playboy, that's no secret. But it only takes one good woman to come along and give him a reason to change. That's the only part of him that you get to have, though. So, if there's anything else about him that you're hoping you can fix or change, you may as well hit the road because it's not gonna happen," he tells me. "Dalton won't leave the MC for you, and he sure as hell won't tell you everything that he does wearing his cut."

"I'm a federal agent and I'm not giving that up either," I reply.

"Good. You shouldn't," he says, surprising me. "And if he loves you, he wouldn't even ask you to do that for him."

"Oh."

"Just like if you love him, you won't ask him to take off the cut. He may even try to do it, but he'd hate you for it. Dalton didn't just join the MC on a whim like most of the guys. He was born into it."

Looking down at the sleeping baby on his shoulder, Torin says, "And if you have a son with him, he'll be a little prince who will most likely want to follow in his father's footsteps and ride like a King one day."

"Dalton's a good guy," I say. "With or without the cut. I know that."

"The question is, can you remember that even when he's not good?" Torin asks.

"All I can do is agree to try."

"That's all any of us can do," he responds with a smirk before he strolls up to us and says, "Come on. I'll walk you over."

We follow him out of the bar, where he locks up and then heads toward the ocean. Like he said, it's easy to spot all of the spotlights shining down on the cage in the pit of a coliseum, with a semi-circle of seats facing the action. The place is packed, almost every seat taken. And I'm not all that surprised when I see the familiar face of the sheriff sitting in the front row. Tonight, she's out of her uniform and in a t-shirt and jeans, a beer in her hand.

"Good to see you making friends in the area, Agent Bradley," Sheriff Horton says when we approach, and she gets to her feet.

"I didn't take you for the fight night kind of girl," I tell her honestly.

"Only when my husband is the headliner," she answers with a grin. "Can't say I pegged you as a fan of MMA either."

"I'm actually looking for Dalton," I tell her. "Have you by chance seen him?"

"He's up at the main gate handling the donations," the sheriff informs me as I look around for him.

"Donations?" I ask when I turn back to her.

"Christmas presents for underprivileged kids," she answers, and Quincey and I exchange a look of shock. "A toy is the price of admission to get into the event tonight."

"The MC isn't all bad," Torin says. "We do a lot of charity work in the community."

"That's...nice," I say.

"But if you hear anything about gambling, the Kings don't know shit about all that," Torin adds with a grin.

"Right," I agree, since that's the least of my concerns. "Quincey, how about you try to find us a seat and I'll go make a donation."

"Sure," she agrees, waving me off as her eyes take in the crowd around us. "Don't mind me. I'll just go get lost in the sea of hot, bearded bikers."

CHAPTER TWENTY-ONE

Dalton

I couldn't tell you how many times I've called Peyton over the last few weeks and she hasn't sent so much as a text message back. But I won't give up. No, I will stay persistent until she says something, dammit.

To try and keep busy, I volunteered to help out with loading up the bus with toys and clothing donations for the local families that can't afford them. Even that work didn't last long. Now that the fight is about to start, everyone's at the concession stand or heading down to find their seats.

I'm on the bus steps, tossing some dolls into the bus, when a woman behind me says, "I don't have any toys, but can I write you a check?"

My neck jerks around so fast it's a wonder I don't get whiplash. Even when I see her, I have to blink a few times to make sure I'm not imagining her.

"Peyton? What are you doing here?" I ask.

"Your calls and flowers finally wore me down," she answers with a smile.

"Fuck, this is so much better than a text message." I jog down the steps to get closer to her. "You're really here," I say as I reach up and cup her face to feel her soft skin.

"Yes, but only if you're serious about us," she tells me when she covers my hand with hers. "I want more than just a few hot nights whenever the mood strikes. I'm too old for hookups and it's too far to keep commuting."

Lowering my hand in disappointment, I say, "I can't move. My dad is here, and the MC..."

"I know," she interrupts. "I wasn't asking you to move. If I'm going to do it, though, I need to know that I can count on you to be around."

"I want you here with me," I tell her. "Fuck, I want to be with you. But you've worked your ass off to have an amazing career, and I can't ask you to give that up."

"I didn't say I would," she replies.

"But you know I'm not leaving the MC either, right?" I ask. "My dad helped start the Savage Kings over twenty years ago. I grew up in the club..."

"I'm aware of all that too," Peyton says.

"So, it sounds like an impossible situation," I grumble.

"Well, I work Monday to Friday, nine to five, right?" she says.

"Yeah."

"So, can you try to handle most of your club business Monday through Friday while I'm at the office?"

Considering that for a moment, I tell her, "Possibly."

"Then, on the weekends, it could just be me and you, no MC and no federal agency responsibilities?" she asks.

"Just us?" I repeat with a grin, liking the idea of this compromise so far. "Peyton and Dalton, a naked superhero duo who only fight bedroom crimes, like sheet hogs and orgasm deficiencies."

Laughing out loud, she says, "That does sound nice, but I'm

going to need more than a secret affair with an outlaw in the bedroom on weekends. I'm asking if we can find a way to go on dates and meet each other's friends and family."

"Oh yeah?" I ask.

"Yeah. And eventually, I'd like to wake up every morning with you and go to bed at night with you. So, no, I don't want to hide you or us. But we can't exactly have our relationship completely out in the open. If my superiors found out about you, I could lose my job."

"Isn't there a federal building near here where you could work?" I ask.

"Once I close the investigation on the Savage Kings, they'll probably send me back to Georgia."

"Maybe not. Could you ask for a more permanent job here?"

"I dunno. I could ask, but there's no guarantee. And the closer I am, the harder it will be for us to keep my superiors from finding out we're together."

"You know I can pull off a pretty good lawyer alter ego," I remind her. "You could tell everyone at work that I'm Henry when you introduce me to them. And I do have forty-nine more of those fancy business cards..."

Peyton blinks at me in confusion for several seconds before she says, "Live a lie, you mean?"

"Only a lie to everyone else. You and I would be the real deal when we're together," I tell her. "I guess you'll have to decide if living a lie is worth being with me because I don't see any other way to make this work, kitten."

"If we do this, if I can figure out a way to work nearby, are you sure you can give up other women?"

"I've already given up women," I assure her. "Ask any of the guys. There hasn't been a woman in my apartment in weeks, since before I started sneaking off to Raleigh to see you. What do you need me to do to prove that? You want a ring on your finger? Because I'll do that!"

"God, no," she says with a wince, as if the idea of marrying me is too awful to even consider. "I've been there, and had a wedding and a ring. Those things won't prevent adultery. I've already learned that lesson."

"So then, what do you need from me?" I ask.

"Honestly, I don't know what it will take before I learn to completely trust you. Maybe I never will because I still don't understand why someone like you would want me."

"I don't know how to prove to you that you're the only woman I want, but I won't stop trying," I promise her. "And I won't do anything to break your trust if you decide that I've earned it. Can you at least believe that?"

"Yes," she whispers.

"Good," I reply before I grab each of her hips and tug her body against mine so I can kiss her lips.

Peyton kisses me back for a moment before she pulls away. "Wait. Aren't you worried about what the MC will think about us? It sounded like your president just gave us his blessing but the rest of them..."

"The club's already voted," I admit. "And they don't care. They were all for it, actually."

"They voted?" she asks. "On us, you and me?"

"Yeah."

"Even though I'm..."

"Even though you're a federal agent and could try to arrest us all one day," I finish for her.

"I won't do that," she tells me.

"Good, because they're more than my friends. Those guys are my family. So, I need to trust you with them, trust that you won't screw us all over if you have to decide between me or your job."

"I won't screw you or the MC over," she assures me, so I give her another kiss.

"I'm glad to hear that," I say against her lips. "Now, would you like to be my date to the fight?"

Smiling broadly up at me, Peyton says, "I would love to."

CHAPTER TWENTY-TWO

Peyton

"Sir, do you have a moment?" I ask Stan Sommers when I pop my head in his office.

"Sure. Come on in," he says. I walk into his office but don't take a seat. I want to say this and get it over with as soon as possible.

"I've finalized my report on the Savage Kings investigation. There's nothing there."

I will myself to believe that but really, I wasn't able to find any direct evidence they were connected to any murders or arson. That doesn't mean there's not any, just that I didn't want to dig deep enough to accidentally find it.

"Oh, well, if you're sure," Stan says in surprise.

"I am," I agree. "Also, there's something else I wanted to speak to you about."

"Yes?"

Taking the plunge, after I spent the entire weekend considering my options, and knowing it's the only way to keep seeing Dalton, I say, "Would it be possible for me to stay on with the Eastern District and work out of the New Bern office, even if it's just an investigator position?"

"New Bern, huh?" he repeats. "You actually *want* to move closer to the Kings? Our CI relocated to California after his identity was blown by them. If he could get a passport, he probably would've left the country."

"My reasons for moving don't have anything to do with the Savage Kings," I lie. "Actually, I've met someone. He's an attorney, in New Bern."

"Really?"

"Yes, and well, the commute is difficult. With email and conference calls, I would be available to your office around the clock for anything you need. You won't even notice that I'm not in the building. And of course, I could attend any meetings or court dates in person as needed."

"I don't see why that would be an issue. We actually need another body in that office anyway. I'll go ahead and start the paperwork for your transfer from Atlanta," he says, without putting up any argument.

"Great. Thank you, sir," I tell him with a smile.

"And I'd love to meet this attorney of yours. Maybe I can stop by and say hello the next time I'm on the coast visiting my niece."

"S-sure," I agree, hoping he doesn't really mean that he would come by our place. Even if he does, I feel confident that Dalton and I can handle it.

Maybe I'm making the biggest mistake of my life, but right now, in this moment, I'm more certain than ever that I want to be with Dalton, come what may.

EPILOGUE

Dalton
A year later...

T onight, I left my bike at the clubhouse since I didn't want to mess up my suit. It's still the only one I own, the one Peyton first fell for me in. I'd hate to fuck it up other than the scuffed knees.

Folding up my cut and putting it away in the saddlebag before I left sucked, but I know for a fact you can take a Savage King out of his patches, but you can never take the patches off of a King.

The bearded skull is a part of me that runs deeper than the ink on my back. It's in my blood and always will be. That's why, every once in a while, I don't mind throwing on some different clothes and playing the part my old lady needs me to play.

Peyton and I have found a way for our polar opposite lifestyles to mesh together. Sometimes she wears leather and sometimes I put on a tie. All that matters is that we know who we are under the clothes we've both chosen to wear in life.

"Honey, I'm home!" I call out after I park my truck in the garage and come in the side door that leads to our kitchen. I start to undo my tie while strolling carefree into the dining room.

"Oh hey, Henry. How was your day? Do you remember me telling you about Assistant U.S. Attorney, Stan Sommers?" Peyton asks when I walk into the room, introducing us like she didn't give me the heads-up last week that he would be stopping by today, so we'd have time to prepare.

"It's such an honor to meet you, sir. Peyton's told me great things," I say to her boss man as I hold out my hand and shake his.

We sit in the living room, shooting the shit for a while, talking mostly about the weather and sports. Turns out, we're both fans of the Wilmington Wildcats football team.

"A few years back, I met two of their wide receivers. Great guys," I say to him.

"You lucky dog," Stan replies with a chuckle.

"Honey, could you help me bring out dinner?" Peyton calls to me from the kitchen.

"Absolutely, kitten. It smells delicious!" I say as I excuse myself and head that way.

In the privacy of our kitchen, I grab my old lady around the waist and kiss her so hard I nearly dip her backwards.

"I want you so much," she whispers against my lips.

"You love Henry the attorney, don't you?" I ask.

Grinning up at me, she says, "I love Dalton, the outlaw biker more. He's a bigger freak in the sheets."

"You don't say?" I ask, giving her another kiss and then the amazing smells hijack my attention. Glancing over to the kitchen island, I see rows of dishes—an entire roasted chicken, mashed potatoes, green beans. There's even fresh bread. "Wow. How long have you been cooking all this? It looks great."

"It's all store-bought," she whispers. "I put it in pots and pans to heat it up and make it look homemade. The containers are out in the garbage bin."

"Damn, kitten. I love it when you pull your own cons. It's so fucking hot." I reach down to squeeze both of her luscious ass cheeks.

"I'm gonna con you out of your suit as soon as dinner is over," she promises with a smile.

"Can't fucking wait," I tell her while slipping my hands up her skirt. When I feel the elastic string of her thong, I give it a tug that makes her panties drop to the floor.

"Dalton!" she whispers as she looks over her shoulder to make sure we're still alone. I bend down to help her lift each of her heels to completely remove the blue lace.

"Knowing you're not wearing panties will make this dinner with your boss even more fun," I assure her, tucking the lace into my pants pocket.

"You're so bad," she tells me with a shake of her head when she turns to grab some plates from the cabinet.

"Yeah, and you fucking love it," I remind her with a smack on her ass.

The End

Reece's book is coming in March! Pre-order here: mybook.to/SKReece

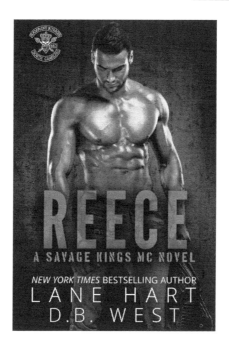

We're also planning books for Miles, Cooper, Sax and Cedric!

ABOUT THE AUTHORS

New York Times bestselling author Lane Hart and husband D.B. West were both born and raised in North Carolina. They still live in the south with their two daughters and enjoy spending the summers on the beach and watching football in the fall.

Connect with D.B.:
Twitter: https://twitter.com/AuthorDBWest
Facebook: https://www.facebook.com/authordbwest/
Website: http://www.dbwestbooks.com
Email: dbwestauthor@outlook.com

Connect with Lane:
Twitter: https://twitter.com/WritingfromHart
Facebook: http://www.facebook.com/lanehartbooks
Instagram: https://www.instagram.com/authorlanehart/
Website: http://www.lanehartbooks.com
Email: lane.hart@hotmail.com

.

Made in the USA
Monee, IL
03 December 2022

19501232R00096